W9-ACW-272

The Mona Lisa
of
Salem Street

Other books by Jan Marino

The Mona Lisa of Salem Street

A Novel by Jan Marino

LITTLE, BROWN AND COMPANY

BOSTON   NEW YORK   TORONTO   LONDON

First Edition

The characters and events in this book are fictitious. Any similarity to
real persons, living or dead, is coincidental and not intended by the author.

Library of Congress Cataloging-in-Publication Data

Marino, Jan.
    The Mona Lisa of Salem Street : a novel / by Jan Marino. — 1st
ed.
        p.   cm.
    Summary: Nettie and John Peter have been passed from one relative
to another ever since their parents died, so when they go to live in
Boston with their grandfather, Nettie doubts he really wants them.
    ISBN 0-316-54614-3
    [1. Brothers and sisters—Fiction.   2. Orphans—Fiction.
3. Grandfathers—Fiction.   4. Boston (Mass.)—Fiction.]   I. Title.
PZ7.M33884Mo   1995
[Fic]—dc20   94-34666

              10 9 8 7 6 5 4 3 2 1

                        RRD-VA

         Printed in the United States of America

For
Justine Elizabeth Marino and Sarah Earl Dealy
with love
and for Mother Courage
with admiration and love

[Family] One of nature's masterpieces.
—*George Santayana*

⊰ CHAPTER ONE ⊱

Nettie liked to think about times long gone. Soft summer evenings at Morgan Creek, John Peter and her father by the shore, stamping bare feet, spraying water almost to where Nettie and her mother sat.

She thought about how her father looked for rainbows in the early evening sky and how her mother sang and told stories. How her father would gather John Peter under one arm, Nettie under the other. "Hush, now," he'd say, squeezing them to him till their heads touched, "Momma's going to sing a story."

Nettie tried hard to remember her mother's stories, so she could sing them to John Peter when he was having trouble sleeping. Sometimes, she'd forget the ending, so she'd make up her own. Didn't matter to John Peter, he liked any story Nettie sang to him. But Nettie always remembered other things about those sweet summer evenings. The best parts. How she felt. All warm and safe. How John Peter smiled, laughed even. How, when the story was over, they would all walk by the edge of the

3

creek toward home. How her father would take John Peter up on his shoulders when John Peter's baby legs got tired.

"Nettie." A hard rap on the bathroom door. "Nettie Dee, you get out of there. You got a heap of things to tend to."

That was Grandma Bessie. Nettie and John Peter had lived with her off and on for most of their lives. Ever since the accident. One day Nettie and John Peter's momma and poppa had been there and then quick, like blowing out birthday candles, they were gone.

"I tried my best," Grandma Bessie said when Nettie came out of the tiny bathroom. "It's not like I shirked my duty."

Nettie spotted John Peter sitting at the kitchen table, chin on his chest, eyes cast down, fighting back tears. Nettie wanted to poke him. She'd told him over and over not to let Grandma Bessie see him cry. "Just like your ma," Grandma Bessie would bellow every time John Peter started up. "Your pa, too. All dreamy and flowery and fancy. Well, it's not my way." Most often she'd give him a swat and pass him a mess of peas to be shelled, or tell him to go out and clean the back pen.

"You hearin' me?" Grandma Bessie's voice and a hard shake brought Nettie's mind to where her body was. In Grandma Bessie's bedroom. "My bones hurt," Grandma Bessie went on. "I'm an old lady. And I like my privacy."

Grandma Bessie *was* old. Everybody knew that. "Poor

Aunt Bessie," Nettie heard Cousin Jen say one day. "She was old when Elizabeth and I were kids. She didn't have much patience then. She's got none now."

Grandma Bessie swung an old duffel bag onto the bed. "Train leaves at noon, and it's costin' me plenty to send you on up there."

She motioned for John Peter to get his suitcase out of the closet.

Nettie and John Peter should have been used to all this. Every time Grandma Bessie got tired of feeding or shoeing them, she'd send them off to another relative.

First there was their mother's cousin, Jen. She'd been nice to them, and Nettie and John Peter got to loving her, but her husband, Renchie, took a dislike to John Peter. Said John Peter made him nervous. Gave him the creeps. "Makes me crazy the way he pokes around, lookin' at stuff he ain't got no business lookin' into." And then he'd go on about the way John Peter looked at him. "Like he's studyin' a map or somethin'."

There was some truth in what Renchie said. John Peter was kind of unsettling to some people. Nettie tried to explain that he didn't mean any harm the way he poked around. And as far as looking at people the way he did, well, that was kind of a family characteristic; it had been said that when their father looked at somebody, it was almost like he was seeing into their very souls.

But the way John Peter poked and looked wasn't the reason Renchie did what he did. Grandma Bessie had promised to send a few dollars a week for their keep, but she never did. And so, one day, just like that, even with Cousin Jen telling Renchie she'd get Grandma Bessie to make good her promise, Renchie packed them into his pickup truck and back they went.

There had been others. Aunt Alice Swann. Cousin Rose Ellen Jensen. Great-uncle Simon. The Digbys. But it was always the same: Grandma Bessie's few dollars never came; Nettie and John Peter never stayed.

The last one they lived with had been Uncle Ben. He'd been Nettie's favorite. He didn't mind her singing. He liked it. He even let her play his old tinny-sounding piano. Nettie liked to pretend that they'd be with Uncle Ben still if he hadn't fallen and broken his two legs. Grandma Bessie blamed John Peter for that. "Fool thing to do. A man his age swingin' from the barn rafters." John Peter tried to explain that Uncle Ben loved to swing and was good at it, but Grandma Bessie told him to shut up. And he did.

From that day on, John Peter hardly spoke to anybody except Nettie, and when he spoke to anybody but Nettie, he stuttered. His face would get all screwed up and his mouth would shake. "I-I-I d-d-d-don't . . . ," he'd say. Grandma Bessie had no patience for that, so Nettie took it upon herself to answer for him.

Grandma Bessie tossed John Peter's underwear into the suitcase. "Your pa's pa is a lot better off than I am. Owns his own business establishment. Frank De-Angelus's Flower Emporium, or some such thing. But you take my word, any emporium business has got to be fancy."

"DeAngelus," Nettie said. "Sometimes I forget that our real name is DeAngelus."

"'Sometimes I forget that our real name is De-Angelus,'" Grandma Bessie mimicked. "You think I was gonna spell out D-E capital A-N-G-E-L-U-S for every fool thing."

Nettie gave John Peter a shove when she saw his chin heading for his chest.

"What about our grandmother DeAngelus?"

"Dead." Grandma Bessie slammed the suitcase shut. "Well, come on. Let's get a move on."

Nettie took her duffel bag, John Peter his suitcase, and they followed Grandma Bessie.

"Now you listen to me," she said as they sat waiting for the train. "It's not like you're goin' up to live with a kid. He's younger than me but he's still up there." She poked John Peter in the ribs when he was momentarily distracted by the hum of the tracks indicating the train was on its way. "You hear me? I said he's up in years. Old. O-L-D." She thumped his ribs again. "And old folks don't have much patience with blubbery little kids who spit all over themselves when they talk." She went on to say that Mr. Frank DeAngelus probably had more money than God. That they'd better mind their p's and q's. And that Nettie better leave her highfalutin' ways right here, where she was sitting. "People like him aren't used to a twelve-year-old twit, nose always in some book, thinkin' she's as smart as a college professor."

The train whistle blew in the distance. Grandma Bessie rattled on. The train pulled in and Nettie and John

Peter boarded. When they were seated, Grandma Bessie's face appeared in the window. "Nettie Dee, don't you go around singin' and tappin' your feet. Folks, especially old ones like him, don't like it."

The train started to move out of the station. But that didn't stop Bessie Whitehall. She ran alongside. "Don't you go tellin' him my business, Nettie. You hear me?"

Nettie heard.

"And don't go pokin' into things that you got no right to poke into." The train picked up speed, Grandma Bessie lost some, but *that* didn't stop her. "That goes for you, too, John Peter. You hearin' me?"

The whole train heard, but John Peter didn't answer.

And the last thing Nettie heard was, "AND REMEM-BER, BOY, NONE OF YOUR BLUBberin' . . ."

⊰ CHAPTER TWO ⊱

Nettie pressed her face to the window and watched all that was familiar to her disappear. It made her sad. Even watching Grandma Bessie fade to a tiny dot. Not that she was really sorry to be leaving — Grandma Bessie had never been really nice to them, or anybody else, for that matter — but Nettie and John Peter had gotten kind of used to her. Kind of even loved her. In all the time they'd been with her, Nettie had only seen her smile when she smoked her evening cigar. Once she'd given John Peter an empty cigar box, the one he kept his treasures in. But most times, if she caught one of them looking at her, her smile would disappear, and she'd tell them to get back to the dishes or tend to some other chore.

Nettie sighed. She sometimes did that. She tried not to, especially in front of Grandma Bessie. "You sighin' like an old lady," she'd say, "him blubberin' like a two-month-old grates on my nerves. Makes me crazy."

"You okay, Nettie?" John Peter asked.

She nodded. "Are you?"

"I feel scared. We've never seen Boston, Massa . . . Massa . . ."

"Massachusetts," Nettie said. "How could we? We've never been out of Ohio." She pulled her duffel bag from under her seat and looked inside. "Good," she said, holding up a tattered book. "At least we can see what it looks like."

"Where'd you get that?"

"Miss Hinton down at the library. They were throwing it away." She opened the book to a map of the United States. "I'll show you where Boston is."

"How far is it?"

Her fingers traveled from Jasper on up through Chillicothe, Columbus, Canton, and on through Pennsylvania and New York.

"There," Nettie said, her finger resting on the coastline of Massachusetts, "that's how far."

She grinned over at him. "And it's on the ocean. We can probably leap right in the water from where we'll be living."

"Nettie," John Peter whispered. "You think it's going to be okay? I mean, you think Mr. DeAngelus is going to like us?"

Nettie wanted to say How should I know? but all she said was "You left out the verb again. It's incorrect to say 'You think Mr. DeAngelus is going to like us?' Say 'Do you think Mr. DeAngelus is going to like us?'"

"Well, will he?"

Nettie again wanted to say How should I know? but she just shrugged and said, "Why not? He's our father's father and our father loved us." She flipped the pages of the book until she came to a picture. "Look, John Peter, this is Ralph Waldo Emerson and this is Henry Thoreau." Before John Peter could ask who they were, Nettie turned the page and let out a tiny gasp. "Oh, how heavenly. Mrs. Isabella Stewart Gardner's Venetian palace on the Fenway." She leaned back, the book resting on her chest. "Oh, John Peter, it's going to be lovely living there."

"It wasn't lovely living with Grandma Bessie and she was our mother's mother and our mother loved us," John Peter said. "Besides, we've never even met our father's father."

"You just don't remember. He came to see us before Poppa and Momma went away."

"How come he stopped coming?"

Nettie sighed a long sigh. "I've told you a million times. Grandma Bessie wouldn't let him."

"So how come she's sending us up there?"

"Because she's run out of people to send us to."

Nettie went back to the book.

"Oh, look, John Peter, isn't this beautiful? It's Louisburg Square." She rested her finger on a picture of a three-story brick house, its tall windows glistening above boxes spilling over with red geraniums, its door knocker gleaming like pure gold. "I just know we'll be living in a house like this."

"How do you know?"

"Because that's where people who have lots of money live." She closed the book carefully. "Grandma Bessie said that Mr. Frank DeAngelus had more money than God." She reached down and tucked the book into her duffel bag.

She shook her head. "We can't call him that." She looked over at John Peter. "We've got to decide what we're going to call him before we get there."

"Call who?"

"Grandfather DeAngelus. We can't go around calling him Mr. DeAngelus." Nettie reached back into her duffel bag and took out two apples. She bit into one and handed John Peter the other. "Do you remember the Trouts over in Fayetteville?"

John Peter shook his head.

Nettie reached out and patted John Peter's hand. "I forgot," she said, "you were only a baby. Well, there was this family named Trout. They were rich, and all the children in the family called their grandfather Grandpère." She took a big bite of the apple. "That means grandfather in French. Doesn't that sound nice? Grandpère."

John Peter shrugged and finished his apple.

"That's what we'll call him," Nettie said, finishing the last of hers. "Grandpère."

"I think that sounds stupid."

"Well, that's what we're going to call him, like it or not."

Nettie took another book from her duffel bag, a small

dictionary she was never without. It was her mother's, and whenever Nettie took it in her hands, closed her eyes, and smelled the leather cover, her mother was there with her. Nettie would run her fingers along the pages, sure that they were resting exactly where her mother's long slim fingers had been.

Nettie opened to the *d*s. "Just as I thought," she said, "*de* means of in French."

"So?"

"So it means that our grandfather's name, our name, means of the angels." She put the book to her lips, kissed it as she always did, closed her eyes, and said, "Of the angels. Oh, it's so lovely. Like the beginning of a beautiful song."

"I think it's dumb."

"Dumb? That's how much you know. Our name has to do with the Deity —"

"The what?"

"The Divinity. God. Do you think God is dumb?"

John Peter shook his head. Hard.

Nettie sat back. "Natasha Allegra DeAngelus." She sighed a long, contented sigh. "Natasha Allegra of the Angels."

"Who's that?"

Nettie turned to John Peter. "Me. That's what I've decided to be called. Natasha Allegra. Natasha means Natalie in Russian and Natalie is my given name, and I've always loved Allegra, laughing Allegra —"

"Laughing who?"

"Allegra. Henry Wadsworth Longfellow's daughter. Laughing Allegra is what he called her in *The Children's Hour*. I think it's perfect. Natasha Allegra." She turned and looked at John Peter square in the eye. "And you, you're going to be J. P. DeAngelus."

"I am not."

"You are, too. 'John Peter' doesn't sound like you come from Boston."

"I don't. Neither do you."

"But we're going to. Educated people live in Boston. Rich people like Grandpère. Do you think they have names like Nettie Dee and John Peter Dee? Well, they don't.

"You may not remember, but I do. Momma always told me if they had to be away for a long time, I was in charge —"

"You were not. Grandma Bessie was."

"Not of everything. Who helped you with your homework? Who did you come to when Grandma Bessie was in one of her I've-got-eyes-behind-my-head moods? When you needed to hear about Momma and Poppa? When you —"

"Okay. Okay. You're in charge."

Nettie slapped his knee. "So if I say you're J.P. and I'm Natasha Allegra, that's who we are. Right?"

John Peter nodded. "You think I'm going to remember to call you that dumb name every single time?"

"You left out the verb again. And it's not a dumb name. It's elegant. And that's what we need. Elegance.

Do you want Grandpère to think we're . . . we're like bumpkins?"

"We are, aren't we?"

"Not anymore. Now what's my name?"

John Peter shook his head.

"Well?"

John Peter sighed a long Nettie sigh. "Natasha Allegra DeAngelus."

"And yours?"

John Peter rolled his eyes. "J.P. J. P. DeAngelus."

Nettie thrust her right hand out. "Very pleased to make your acquaintance, J. P. DeAngelus." She shook his hand hard. "Natasha Allegra at your service."

⚔ CHAPTER THREE ⚔

The night passed slowly. It was difficult for Nettie and John Peter to get comfortable, even though the kindly conductor gave them pillows and blankets and permission to use two double seats.

John Peter checked the contents of his cigar box. Nettie stared out into the darkness. The train's whistle blew as the train roared through small towns. Lights flickered in distant houses. Nettie imagined her mother and father in one of those houses. Her father building a fire, her mother singing as she baked honey cakes. Nettie filling a jar with daisies to place on the table. John Peter laughing.

A hollow feeling come over Nettie, almost like when she hadn't eaten for a long while. But that wasn't so. She had fixed bologna sandwiches and apple juice for their supper. They'd even had cookies. That had surprised John Peter.

"You sleeping, Nettie?"

Nettie didn't answer.

"Nettie," he said again, louder, "you think Grandma Bessie misses us?"

Still no answer.

"She put cookies in for us, maybe she's sorry she sent us away."

Nettie wanted to tell him that she was the one who had put the cookies in, that she'd sneaked them out of the cupboard. The apple juice, too.

"Nettie, please."

"Shhhhhh," the lady across the aisle hissed. "People are trying to sleep."

"S-s-s-s-sorry."

"Nettie," John Peter whispered, "talk to me. Please."

Still Nettie didn't answer.

"Natasha Allegra, I'm scared."

Natasha Allegra didn't answer.

Right now, here, on this train, Nettie was tired of comforting him. Tired of always protecting him. Tired of making him feel things would be all right. Because now, in a darkened train, on her way to a stranger in a strange place, she wasn't sure anything would ever be all right. When John Peter whispered her name again, Nettie pretended to be asleep, the same way she pretended lots of things, sometimes so long and so hard, she got to believing. Like the way she believed Momma and Poppa would came back. That after the accident they were taken to a beautiful place high in the mountains of Montana with people to care for them. That the accident had given them amnesia and they couldn't remember who they were. Not yet. But one day they'd come and Poppa would lift John Peter to his shoulders and head toward the creek, Nettie and Momma trotting along behind.

For a time, when Nettie needed somebody to comfort her, to know things would be all right, she'd go off by herself and talk to them. Until Grandma Bessie heard her. "How many times have I got to tell you, you pray for the dead, you don't talk to them. 'Less you want your head to go soft as Beau Grenville's."

That had scared Nettie. Everyone in Jasper knew Beau wasn't right. "He ought to be locked up, the way he goes around dressed like Teddy Roosevelt, telling folks how he calls the White House every morning to check in with President Clinton," people would say.

Ever since then, Nettie stopped talking to her mother and father. She didn't pray for them either, because that would mean she'd never see them again. She did pray to God, but sometimes she didn't get the answer when she needed it. Like now. She needed to know if her grandfather would like them and let them stay, or if he'd ship them back to Grandma Bessie, who would ship them off to somebody else. Nettie hated that. It was humiliating, being packed up again and again.

Nettie never told anybody how she felt about that. Not even John Peter. She pretended it didn't matter. But it did matter. Every time they got sent somewhere, Nettie tried so hard to get people to love her and John Peter. She did everything they told her to do. She helped with chores when she wasn't even asked. And she let herself love them. Even Renchie. But still, in the end, it was always the same. This time had to be different because Grandpère had lots of money and wouldn't need Grandma Bessie's few dollars.

But deep down Nettie knew it might not be different. She remembered how Grandma Bessie said the rich, even though they held a loaf of bread in each hand, complained of being hungry. And Nettie had read enough to know that having money didn't always mean that you were kind and good to children. Fraülein Rottenmeier had been hateful to Heidi. David Copperfield's stepfather had whipped him and sent him away.

Nettie promised herself that she and John Peter would do everything right, just the way they had with everybody they'd ever lived with. They would do all that was asked of them, and more. And then she promised herself something else. She wouldn't let them love Grandpère. Not until she was sure — very, very, very sure — he'd let them stay.

Nettie heard John Peter whimper. *Well, just let him. He's eight years old now, he's no baby.*

Another whimper.

I can't do everything, God. I'm only twelve, that's not so old. Ellie Lockwood's mother still fusses with her hair, and Ellie's almost thirteen.

A sob.

Tell him to stop. But John Peter didn't.

Nettie turned and put her arm around him. She knew

his face was wet and sticky even though she couldn't see it clearly.

"Natasha" . . . sob . . . "Allegra —"

Nettie softened the way she always did with John Peter. "You don't have to call me that when we're alone. Just when we're in Boston and people are around. Okay?"

"Okay," he mumbled.

"Do you know how they pronounce the place where we're going to live?"

"How?"

"Lou-is-burg, not Lou-ee-berg, Square. Bostonians say it the English way, not the French way." Nettie tucked the blanket around him. "You'll see, everything's going to be fine," she whispered, stumbling on her own words. "Just fine."

The train roared on and when the first light of day filtered through the window, the conductor called out, "Back Bay Station next stop. Last stop is South Station." He leaned over and smiled at Nettie and John Peter. "That's your stop. We'll be there in about half an hour. Give you time to get yourselves some breakfast." He winked at them. "Don't forget your valuables when you leave."

Nettie made sure they washed up real good. She checked John Peter's teeth, combed his hair, and made him put on fresh socks and underwear. She put on a clean blouse and tried to fix her hair, but it was impossible, the curls just wouldn't cooperate. John Peter fussed about wanting to go to the dining car to get some hot chocolate, but Nettie didn't want to spend any of the fifteen dollars Grandma Bessie had given her. "See that you don't spend this unless you have to," Grandma Bessie had said. "He don't need my money, so send it back when you get there."

They finished up the bologna sandwiches and when the last of the apple juice was gone, John Peter asked for a cookie.

"They're gone," Nettie said. "I'm sorry."

John Peter shrugged. "That's okay." He gathered the leavings of breakfast and took them to the trash bin at the end of the car.

When he got back, the two of them sat quietly until the conductor called out "South Station." Then John Peter said in a very small voice, "She must have liked us a little, else she wouldn't have sent those cookies. Right, Nettie?"

Nettie wanted to say, "Wrong, wrong, wrong," but all she did was nod and say, "That's right, John Peter." She carefully tucked her dictionary into her duffel bag, told John Peter to put his cigar box into his suitcase, and then she took his hand, held it real tight, and headed toward where they had to go.

⊰ Chapter Four ⊱

Nettie and John Peter walked slowly down the station platform into the huge glass building where they were to meet their grandfather.

"He'll meet you at the information booth. If the train's early and he's late, you make sure you stay by that booth till he comes," Grandma Bessie had warned.

Holding John Peter's hand, Nettie made her way through the crowds of people. They passed stands selling coffee and pastries, stalls filled with flowers, a pizza parlor, before finally coming to the information booth. But there was nobody waiting. Just more crowds of people coming and going.

Nettie settled John Peter on a nearby bench, telling him to watch the baggage and warning him not to move or speak to anyone. "I'm going back to the information booth." She stood there waiting, one watchful eye on the booth, the other on John Peter, hoping their grandfather would come soon, wondering when he did come if she'd recognize him. It had been a long time since she'd seen him. She'd asked Grandma Bessie before they left Jasper what he looked like, but all she'd answer was, "Can't say. Only saw a picture of him and half his head was chopped off."

Nettie looked up at the clock. It was eleven o'clock; almost an hour had passed since they'd come. An uneasy feeling started in Nettie's chest. She took a deep breath, let it out slowly, and went back to where John Peter sat. His cigar box was on his lap, his key chain clutched in his hand. Nettie hated to look at that chain, especially the keys hanging from it. It had been their father's, and the keys were the keys to the house they'd lived in. "You're going to lose that if you keep taking it out," Nettie said. "Put it back." But he didn't. He clutched it harder.

The big clock on the wall ticked on. Still they sat, John Peter fingering his keys, Nettie's eyes glued to the information booth. People came and went, calling out, "Hello, you little sweetheart" and "Did you have a good trip?" and "Good to see you." But their grandfather didn't come.

Eleven-thirty. Eleven forty-five. And when the noon whistle blew, Nettie poked John Peter. "I see him. I see Grandpère."

John Peter leapt up, spilling the key chain and his cigar box to the ground. "Where?" he shouted.

"There," Nettie whispered, pointing to a tall elegant man with a silvery-gray hat. The heavy feeling she'd had in her chest lifted somewhat. "You wait here," she said, scooping up John Peter's treasures and placing them in his hands. "I'll be right back." Taking a few steps, she turned, pulled herself up to her full five-foot-two-inch height, her positive spirit flooding back to her, and said, "What's your name?"

"John Peter —"

"But what are you called?"

"J.P."

"And I am?"

"Natasha Allegra of the —"

Nettie gave him a quick nod, then turned to continue toward Grandpère, but he had disappeared. She walked around, looked everywhere, but he was gone.

Walking back to where John Peter waited, Nettie sighed a deep sigh. "Put those keys away. Please."

John Peter opened his cigar box and slipped them inside.

"What if he never comes?"

"Don't be silly. He'll be here." But Nettie wasn't sure of that. She wasn't sure of anything. Maybe Grandma Bessie had forgotten to tell him where to meet them. She was always forgetting things. But maybe she *hadn't* forgotten. Maybe he *wouldn't* come because he didn't want them. Maybe he'd told Grandma Bessie just that, and Grandma Bessie had sent them anyway.

The clock ticked all the way to three o'clock, and still Nettie and John Peter sat.

"I'm hungry, Nettie," John Peter said for the hundredth time. "And I'm getting scarederer."

"There's no such word as *scarederer*. It's *scared*. That's what you are. Scared." Nettie was scared, too, so scared she wanted to cry, but all she did was tell John Peter to get his suitcase and follow her.

John Peter's chin began to quiver.

"What's the matter? All I said was to follow me —"

"But what if he comes and we're not where we're supposed to be?"

"We can't just sit here."

John Peter's chin headed for his chest. "Do we have enough money to go back to Ohio?"

"Ohio? We're not going back to Ohio. I'm going to call him."

John Peter's eyes filled up. "If he didn't come for us, maybe he doesn't want —"

"Stop that." She reached into her pocket and handed him a tissue. "Help me. Don't cry." Then, her voice softening, "It'll be okay. It will. I promise."

But when Nettie dialed the number written on the slip of paper Grandma Bessie had stuffed into her pocket, there was no answer, and the panic Nettie had been fighting began to take over. *What am I supposed to do? We can't stay here. It's going to get dark and John Peter is afraid of the dark. Please, God, please, somebody tell me what to do.*

"When is he coming?"

Nettie took a deep breath. "He's not coming." She motioned for John Peter to follow her. "We're going."

"Where?"

"To four-sixty-one Salem Street."

25

John Peter stumbled along after Nettie, dragging his suitcase behind him, asking her over and over questions she had no answers to.

Outside a cold rain fell. Trucks and buses sounded their horns. People pushed their way to the curb, shouting out to passing taxis.

Nettie slung her duffel bag over her shoulder and yanked John Peter's arm. "Come on," she said, making her way to the curb, waving to a taxi heading their way. The driver leaned across the seat and asked where they were going.

"Salem Street. Four-sixty-one Salem Street."

"Hop in the back," he said, "I'll throw your bags in the trunk."

John Peter stood, cigar box in hand, and refused to get in. "Remember what Cousin Jen said," he whispered into Nettie's ear. "You're not supposed to get in strange cars with strange people."

"But this isn't a strange car. It's a taxi and he's the driver."

"Come on, kid, get in. You think I got all day?"

"I-I-I-I-I'm n-n-n-not getting in."

"Well, *I* am," Nettie said. "You can stay here for all I care." The anxiety that had been building up was hard to hold down, but Nettie managed. "I mean it, John Peter," she said in one final, desperate attempt to get him into the taxi. "I'm leaving."

She got into the taxi. John Peter stood his ground for about two seconds before the driver picked him up and plopped him into the back of the taxi. "I'm harmless," he said. "I've got five kids. Two dogs. My wife is a parole officer. And I'm registered with the union."

Maneuvering in and out of traffic, the taxi reached the main street. Once there, the driver pressed a lever on the fare box, put the radio on, and slapped the wheel in time to the music.

Nettie felt sick to her stomach. Grandma Bessie had only given her fifteen dollars and already the fare box read $1.50. She tried to ask how far Salem Street was, but when the driver wasn't slapping the wheel he was on the two-way radio telling somebody where he was and asking the somebody where he was to pick up his next fare.

John Peter kept poking her, telling her they were passing the tallest building in the world or they were passing a statue of somebody or other. How he never saw such skinny streets with carts piled high with fruits and vegetables. But Nettie saw nothing except the rising fare.

She held her breath when the meter clicked to six dollars and didn't breathe again until the driver said, "You're here. Four-sixty-one Salem Street."

Old buildings lined both sides of the narrow street. Nettie saw signs for Hector's Bakery, the Salem Street Meat Market, Umberto's Sweet Shop. And at number four-sixty-one, across a dingy storefront window, loomed a sign that set Nettie's heart pounding: "DeAngelus and Son Funeral Parlor."

Funeral Home? DeAngelus and Son? Was that for Poppa? The anxiety took hold of her.

"Nettie," John Peter whispered, "I lost my keys."

"Didn't I tell you to keep them in the box?" Nettie was surprised to hear her own voice. It sounded like Grandma Bessie's. But out it came again. "Well, didn't I?"

John Peter's chin headed for his chest.

"Don't start. I'll find them."

Nettie turned and frantically moved her hands between the seat cushions.

"Let's move it," the driver said, poking his head in the window, "I've got a pickup in three minutes."

Nettie's hands moved faster. "I've got them," she said, handing them to John Peter. "Put them away. Now. And don't you dare cry." She pushed him toward the door and handed the driver Grandma Bessie's ten-dollar bill. "Are you sure this is four-sixty-one Salem Street? My grandfather owns a flower shop, not a funeral parlor."

He looked around. "Unless they pulled a fast one when I wasn't looking, this is Salem Street." Putting their bags on the curb, he counted out Nettie's change, wished them luck, and took off.

Grandma Bessie lied. Telling us our grandfather was rich. Telling us he owned a big flower business.

Nettie tried to look into the window, but it was so dirty the only thing she could see was piles of long boxes.

"Josie," someone called. "You be sure he grinds it fresh. Don't let him sell you yesterday's meat." Across the street, a woman with long dark hair was at a window calling to a girl standing beneath her on the sidewalk. "Mama," the girl called back. "I heard you fifty times."

Nettie's mind began to race. As terrible as some of the places they'd been sent to had been, this was the worst. A funeral home. *Does it mean there are bodies inside? Does it mean we'll be sleeping in the same house with dead people? How could I have imagined living in Louisburg Square? With window boxes and golden door knockers. To dream of being at Mrs. Jack Gardner's Venetian palace. How could I be so stupid to believe Grandma Bessie? All she wanted to do was to get rid of us once and for all.*

A cold shiver ran down Nettie's spine. Dead people. She had never seen a dead person.

"Nettie. Come on." John Peter pulled on her arm. "We're here."

"But it's a funeral home. I'm not staying in a funeral home."

He shrugged.

It was strange. John Peter was afraid of so many things, but when Cousin Renchie's grandfather died and Grandma Bessie demanded they pay their respects, he didn't mind. "May his soul and those of all...," Grandma Bessie recited on the long walk to the funeral home. John Peter went all the way, even knelt by the coffin. But Nettie didn't. She ran off and waited beneath the porch for the wrath of Grandma Bessie to descend upon her.

He tugged at her sleeve. "We've got nowhere else to go, Nettie."

He was right. Nettie had exactly six dollars and eighty

cents. She took a deep breath, then motioned for John Peter to pick up his bag. She pushed open the heavy door, its green paint chipped and worn, and read the sign hanging on the inner door: "DeAngelus and Son Funeral Parlor and Office — Residence Two Floors Above." She started up the dim, narrow staircase, the tin walls and ceiling echoing their footsteps, and when she saw the sign, "Residence: DeAngelus and Son," she reached out for John Peter's hand, took a very deep breath, and pushed the buzzer. Hard.

-=i Chapter Five ﾚ-

As soon as the door opened, the small, dreary hallway was filled with the smell of furniture polish mixed with a queer, burning aroma.

A man holding a broom stood in the doorway. Nettie tightened her hand around John Peter's. The man looked nothing like her father. Her father was thin and just tall enough for her mother's head to rest on his shoulder. His hair was silky and red, like John Peter's; his eyes brown, like hers. This man was so tall the top of her mother's head, even if she were on her tiptoes, would not come anywhere near his shoulder. And he was more than thin. He was as skinny as the knife grinder who came through Jasper every spring. The one Grandma Bessie said she could slip under a door.

This man's steel-color hair stuck up like straight pins; his eyes were set deep in a face that was one big frown. And he wasn't old. At least not as old as Grandma Bessie said he was. Relief surged through Nettie. *This is not our grandfather.*

But when he looked at her, really looked at her, she knew it was. His eyes were like her father's. Not the color, not the shape, and not the way they almost disappeared behind thick, dark eyelashes. It was the way they seemed to see beyond hers. He took a deep breath; the frown deepened. "Is there something I can do for —" He propped the broom against the wall and looked up. "I know. I know," he said, his voice barely above a whisper. "No matter what Bessie said, I should not have allowed them to travel alone."

Nettie tried to peer behind him to see who he was talking to, but there was nobody there.

He reached out and took their bags. "Come in. Come in. How did you get here?"

"We took a taxi," Nettie said.

He looked up again. "My head is not with me." He dropped their bags inside the door, excused himself, and rushed from the room. Holding a piece of paper, he came back to where Nettie and John Peter stood. "Ah," he said, pointing to the paper, "your grandmother Bessie gave me the wrong day. She writes, 'They will arrive at South Station on February ninth' —" His face paled.

"Today *is* the ninth," Nettie said.

"How can that be?" He looked over at John Peter. "Are you sure you were not to come on the tenth?"

John Peter shook his head.

"I am sorry. Very sorry." He picked up the broom. "I was preparing for tomorrow today. I have cooked a special supper —" He left the room again. "*Dio mio,* I did it again. I burned the sauce."

32

How could this be her father's father? Living in a funeral parlor. Not knowing when they were to arrive. Forgetting what he was cooking. Talking to somebody who wasn't there.

Nettie looked around at the sunless parlor. A worn rug, dark red and patterned, a sofa, some chairs, pictures tilted this way and that. She looked into the kitchen to where the grandfather stood over the stove, steam swirling around his head. The refrigerator was squeezed in between the sink and the stove. The table was in the center of the floor, three chairs around it; an orange cat, its fluffy tail coiled around its skinny body, sat beneath.

Nettie folded her arms and sighed. Somewhere deep inside her, she had known that this was what it would be like. Small. Crowded. Gloomy. But nowhere inside her did she imagine it would be a funeral home.

"The sun is here in the morning." The grandfather's words startled Nettie. "Your grandmother liked the morning best." He put the pot he was holding in the sink, looked at Nettie, and smiled a small, crooked smile. "You favor her. You have her soft brown eyes and the curls she never could tame." He nodded. "You are as beautiful as she was, Nettie —"

"Sh-she's n-not Nettie. She's N-natasha Allegra and I-I'm J-J-J.P."

Nettie could hardly believe what she heard. John Peter actually talking to somebody without poking her or whispering what he wanted to say. And of all things to say. This wasn't the place to be Natasha Allegra and J.P.

The grandfather looked puzzled but said, "Those are fine names."

"And w-w-we're going to c-c-call you —"

Nettie stepped on his foot. Hard.

"What'd you do that for?" John Peter howled, bending down to rub his foot.

"Sorry." Nettie stooped down, pretending to comfort him. "Don't say Grandpère," she whispered. "Please."

"Are you all right?" the grandfather asked.

"He's fine," Nettie said. "Aren't you?"

John Peter nodded.

"Now then, you must be hungry," the grandfather said. He seemed uneasy. Nervous almost. He sat down and motioned for Nettie and John Peter to join him. *"Sedetevi.* Sit. What can I get for you?"

Nettie remained standing. "Nothing, thank you."

"A little snack?"

"Nothing, thank you."

"And you, J.P.?"

John Peter looked over at Nettie. "N-n-nothing, th-thank you," he answered, shaking his head.

"A cool drink? Lemonade?"

Nettie shook her head.

Again, he looked over at John Peter. Again, John Peter shook his head.

The grandfather repeated how sorry he was for not having met them, trying to explain how it might have happened. How, ever since his Anna died, he had a habit of repeating to himself things he must remember. How he had repeated over and over the day and time they were to arrive. But perhaps he had repeated "the tenth at nine" instead of "the ninth at ten," because when he had looked at Grandma Bessie's letter again, he himself had been surprised when he read they would arrive on the ninth. He looked up. "But they are here now."

"A-anybody c-can f-forget."

"Thank you, J.P.," the grandfather said, looking down at the flowered oilcloth. "I am glad you children have come." He rubbed a worn spot. "Since your grandmother is gone I forget everything. Last week I forgot where I put my glasses and put on one black shoe and one brown."

John Peter laughed. Actually laughed. Like he'd been here forever. But Nettie didn't. It wasn't funny forgetting to meet them, like they were just another pair of glasses. And his being glad they were here, well, Nettie knew that didn't mean too much. She and John Peter had heard that before. Lots of times.

The grandfather's frown lifted a little. "That is the first time somebody has laughed in this kitchen since Anna is gone. It was good to hear.

"And now," he said, pushing himself away from the table, "it is time you get settled, to see where you will sleep. And it is time I call Bessie to let her know you have arrived safely." Nettie knew it wouldn't matter to Grandma Bessie where they were, as long as it wasn't with her. And it didn't matter to Nettie where she slept because she wouldn't be sleeping. Not in a funeral home.

She dutifully followed John Peter and the grandfather down the long, dreary hallway lined with all sorts of old, dusty photographs and into a bedroom as tiny as the sleeping compartments she'd seen on the train.

"This was your father's room. It is just the way he left it," the grandfather said, his voice trailing off.

Nettie looked at the faded wallpaper, the worn maple chest of drawers, the old brass bed covered with a thin chenille spread. A limp doll dressed like a bride sat on the bed.

"M-my f-father had a doll?" John Peter asked.

He did it again, Nettie thought. John Peter spoke.

"No," the grandfather said, picking up the doll, "this was your grandmother's." He looked over at Nettie. "Anna would want her granddaughter to have this, Natasha."

Before Nettie could say she really didn't want to be called Natasha, he said in a very soft voice, "Natasha suits you."

He handed the doll to her, then looked over at John Peter. "Perhaps Cassie will sleep with you."

"Wh-wh-who is that?"

"My cat. The one who sits and sleeps and does little else."

The grandfather lifted Nettie's bag onto the bed. "I put some of your grandmother's crocheted hangers in your closet."

The closet wasn't hers, Nettie knew that. Nothing was ever hers. But it never mattered, because they never stayed. And it would be the same here. She wanted to tell him that, but all she said was a quiet thank-you.

The grandfather led John Peter across the hall and into the tiniest room of all. "I apologize for the disorder but each time I begin to clean it, I cannot get rid of anything that was your grandmother's."

"Th-that's okay," John Peter said, "I-I l-like to keep things, too. I-I k-k-keep them in my c-c-cigar box."

"What a good thing to do."

From across the hall, Nettie listened. John Peter never, ever felt comfortable with people he hardly knew. And here he was talking, telling a stranger, well, practically a stranger, about his cigar box. Nettie was puzzled. Puzzled about how she felt about his speaking up, stuttering and all. She sometimes felt annoyed when he'd poke her and whisper what he wanted to say. But now, there was a different feeling.

"C-can I-I ask you something?" she heard John Peter say.

"Of course."

"D-d-do you have d-d-dead bodies here?"

"No," the grandfather said. "That used to be our business, your grandmother's and mine. And it was a good one. But since she is gone, I have no heart for anything." He cleared his throat. "Now, come, let me help you get settled."

Nettie heard some shuffling around and then heard the grandfather say that he thought it best to close the door. "It will give us a bit more room to move around."

Nettie was relieved that there were no dead bodies around, but the way he talked about them upset her. A good business, he'd said. Like he was in the toy business. Nettie sighed one of her long sighs and went over to the window.

She looked out at the other buildings. Like old shoe boxes stacked on top of one another. All the same, except the one with the lady at the window. She reminded Nettie of the picture on the old calendar that hung on the back of her mother's closet at Grandma Bessie's.

"Josie," the lady called. "Get your brother. It's almost time for supper."

Her voice was loud, but her words were gentle, the way Nettie remembered her mother's voice calling to John Peter. The grandfather's voice broke Nettie's thoughts. "You take all the time you need. Supper will be ready soon."

As soon as his footsteps faded, Nettie crossed over to John Peter and closed the door behind her. "I couldn't hear anything. What was he talking about?"

"He said he didn't have any dead people here."

"I heard that part. What else did he say?"

"That his business was very bad. Terrible."

"I heard that, too."

"Did you hear the part about Aleta?"

Nettie shook her head. "Who's Aleta?"

"Our great-aunt. Poppa's aunt. Our grandmother's baby sister."

"Baby sister?"

"That's what he said. He said she was the makeup lady at the funeral home and he's supposed to take care of her."

"Why should he take care of her?"

John Peter shrugged.

"What else did he say?"

"He said he lost his heart and that we could call him Pa. He said Poppa called him Pa."

"Well, I'm not calling him Pa."

"Why not?"

Nettie opened the door and went across the hall.

John Peter followed.

"You didn't answer me and that's rude."

"I'm thinking about other things."

"Like what?"

"I'll tell you when I've thought everything through."

"You know what I think? I think Pa's face isn't like him."

"What are you talking about?"

"Well, his face looks grouchy, like he can't smile. But he's not grouchy. And you know what else I think?"

Nettie didn't answer.

"I think he's nice."

"You know him for all of five minutes and he's nice? What's the matter with you? Don't you know you can't tell anything about a person in five minutes?"

John Peter shrugged. "But he's not just a person. He's our grandfather."

Nettie paid no attention but gathered up the last of her belongings and put them in the dresser drawer even though she knew it was a waste of time.

"You know what else? I think I'm going to like it here."

Nettie still paid no attention.

John Peter sat on the edge of the bed. "You should try to like it here, too."

Nettie whirled around and faced him. "What does it matter? What does it matter to anybody what I like? Did it matter to Grandma Bessie? Or Jen or Uncle Ben? Sure, Jen was nice, so was Uncle Ben, but did anybody keep us? Did they ask us where we wanted to be? No. They just sent us back to Grandma Bessie like we're boomerangs to get tossed somewhere, always landing back where we came from."

She turned and closed the dresser drawer, and with her back to John Peter she said, her voice low, "It's going to be the same here, so please don't get to thinking it's going to be different."

"But Natasha Allegra —"

"Don't call me that."

"But you said —"

"I know I did, but don't."

John Peter went over and put his hand on Nettie's arm. "Pa is making us supper."

Nettie shook her head. "You're doing it again."

"Doing what?"

"Calling him Pa and getting all comfortable —"

"But he told me to call him that. You want me to call him Grandpère?"

Again, Nettie shook her head. "No," she said, her chin quivering. "He's not Grandpère. And this isn't Fayetteville. And we most definitely are not the Trouts."

⊰ Chapter Six ⊱

"Supper is almost ready," the grandfather called from the kitchen.

"You go," Nettie said, "I'm not hungry."

"I don't want to go alone."

"Go ahead." She turned and looked out the narrow window beside the bed. "You don't need me."

"I do too need you," John Peter said, his voice almost breaking. "Please, Nettie —"

She didn't answer.

"Please, Natasha —"

She turned quickly. "I told you not to call me that, didn't I?"

His chin headed for his chest.

As always, Nettie softened. She came over and sat beside him. "Listen to me. If Grandma Bessie didn't send Cousin Jen and all the rest money, she's not going to send him any. She thinks he's rich."

"We could tell her he's not —"

"That won't make any difference."

"Maybe his business will get good again."

She stood up. "Well, if that happens we couldn't stay. We can't live in a funeral home. You know what that will be like?"

"Now you left out the verb."

"Don't change the subject. It would be eerie. Spooky. Scary. Like living with ghosts."

"I don't mind. I liked it when Miss Onthank picked me to be the spirit of Christmas yet to come and I wore a sheet and told Scrooge he died —"

"Will you stop?"

"— and when I told him that Tiny Tim could live if he'd —"

"Forget about Tiny Tim. Forget about Scrooge. And whether you like ghosts or not, we're not staying."

"You're getting mean, Nettie. Real mean."

"I'm trying to make you understand something. Don't you remember, when it didn't work out with Cousin Jen, we were sure Aunt Alice Swann would never let us go back to Grandma Bessie. Remember how she always said, 'How could that woman give up her precious treasures.' But we weren't so precious, because Aunt Alice gave us back. Same as Uncle Ben and all the rest."

"Uncle Ben would have kept us if he hadn't broken his legs."

"I never told you this, but even before he broke his legs, I knew he was going to send us back —"

"But you always said Uncle Ben would have kept us —"

"That's the way I used to be. Always thinking the best." She sighed. "But that's over." She took John Peter's hand. "Now listen to me. While we're here, we'll do everything we're asked to do. And even things we're not asked to do. But please, don't let yourself love it. And most especially, don't get to love him."

John Peter pulled his hand away. "I don't think he's like all the rest. He won't send us back —"

"That's wishful thinking and it won't get us anywhere. Remember what Grandma Bessie always said: 'Put your wishes in a thimble and a mess of peas in a twenty-gallon pot and see what gets filled up first.' "

"What does that mean?"

"It means that wishes don't come true."

"Some do. Besides, I like him."

"It's all right to like him. That's okay. Just don't love him. It'll hurt too much."

"Maybe we won't."

"Maybe we won't what?"

"Leave."

"You haven't listened to one thing I've said. I'm telling you one last time. We won't be staying. It just won't happen. Do you understand?"

John Peter nodded a limp nod.

"Supper is ready. Come before it turns cold."

Nettie handed John Peter a tissue. "Remember what Grandma Bessie told you about blubbering."

John Peter forced a smile. "And poking around."

"And poking, too."

"Come, children." A loud call from the kitchen. "Suppertime."

"Blow your nose," Nettie said, passing him another tissue. She put her arm around him, and the two of them walked down the long, dreary hallway, past pictures of people long gone, and into the grandfather's kitchen.

⊰ Chapter Seven ⊱

The grandfather was at the sink, the steam rising from the pasta he was draining enveloping his head. Cassie, the cat, was at the window, her head resting on the sill, her paw stretched out through the narrow opening onto the fire escape.

John Peter went over and rubbed her fur. She meowed but didn't move. "Who is she looking for?"

The grandfather shrugged. "Pigeons, mostly, but there are times I think she waits for Anna to pass by."

Nettie didn't think the cat was waiting for Anna. The grandfather had burned the sauce, and she had noticed burn marks on the chest of drawers and a charred pipe on the hall table. Nettie was convinced the cat was sitting there in case of a fire.

The grandfather stirred and tasted, lifted the pot from the stove to the counter, and motioned for them to sit down. "I have not cooked this way in a long time.

"How I used to love Sunday night suppers with

Anna," he said, piling plates with macaroni. "She would make the sauce and I would fix the salad. Her sauce was like nectar from the gods."

Nettie waited for him to look up and ask Anna if that wasn't so, but all he did was pour what looked like melted butter on top of their macaroni. "This is *olio d'oliva,* olive oil with garlic and lots of good cheese," he said, placing a dish at each place.

He passed bread and salad, said a little prayer, and they began their meal. Nettie barely ate. John Peter finished two plates of macaroni, and when that was gone, he ate the salad, and when the salad was gone, he ate the rest of the bread.

The grandfather looked up. "He eats like our John."

When John Peter had finished the last of the bread, the grandfather began to clear the table. Nettie got up to help and told John Peter to do likewise, but the grandfather said they were to sit down, that it was a very special night, and that they were about to celebrate. "Cappuccino for everybody." He looked over at the cat. "Is that right, Cassie?" He waited a minute and then said, "Of course it is."

Nettie sighed a quiet sigh. He talked to the cat, too. Even answered for her. Nettie could imagine what Grandma Bessie would say. "Another Beau Grenville."

The cappuccino machine hissed and sizzled, and when it stopped, the grandfather poured the hot, steaming liquid into each of the cups he had placed on the table.

Nettie had never seen anything like it. It smelled like

chocolate and coffee but looked like a cup of whipped cream. "Have you ever had cappuccino?" And before either of them could answer, he said, "Every time I have a cup, I think of old Mr. Gabese. When we buried his mother, he had no money to pay us, so he gave us this." He patted the cappuccino machine. "'Joseph,' my Anna said to him the day he brought it to us, 'this is not necessary.' And she meant it. But she knew what a proud man he was, so she took it." He looked up. "You always knew what was right." Then he sprinkled what looked like cinnamon in each cup and placed one at his feet. "Come, Cassie, time to celebrate."

John Peter looked over at Nettie. She rolled her eyes.

The grandfather picked up his cup, held it up, and said, "And now for a toast." He reached out and lightly touched Nettie's cup, then John Peter's, and finally the cat's. "To my grandchildren." He put the cup to his lips but didn't drink. "To Mr. Gabese." And then very softly, "And to you, Anna."

He took a sip, then asked them how they liked it. "It was your father's favorite."

John Peter drank his and announced it was his favorite, too. But Nettie, determined not to like anything very much, said politely, "It's very nice."

The grandfather smiled and drank deeply. When the last of his cappuccino was gone, he looked over at Nettie, then John Peter, raised his eyes, and said, very, very softly, "Do not worry. I will try my best."

⇥ CHAPTER EIGHT ⇤

It took Nettie a long, long while to get to sleep. At first she thought it was the cappuccino. But when the hall clock chimed midnight, she knew it wasn't. She thought about what the grandfather had said about trying his best. That's what Grandma Bessie said the day she put them on the train. "I tried my best." *What did it mean to try your best? It was* doing *your best. That's what really mattered.*

Nettie had told John Peter she'd tell him a story, the way she always did, but by the time she was ready, he had fallen asleep. With all his clothes on. He sometimes did that, but Nettie would always rouse him and help him undress. She tried to do it tonight, but he pushed her away. "Too tired. Want to sleep," he muttered. He wouldn't even let her take off his shoes.

Then a while later the grandfather made his way down the hall and into where John Peter slept. Nettie watched as John Peter let the grandfather undress him, watched as he put the covers around him, watched as he stood over John Peter until he fell back into a deep sleep.

Nettie pretended she was asleep when the grandfather came into her. She lay still, made sure her breath was slow and even as he pulled the covers up around her. He stood over her for a long time and before he left, he touched her forehead lightly and whispered something to Anna that Nettie couldn't hear.

Nettie listened as he walked down the hall toward his room, and when she heard his door close, she opened her eyes and looked across the hall at John Peter. He had never let anybody but Nettie undress him before. Once when Aunt Alice Swann had tried to help him unzip his stuck zipper, he had clutched it so hard his knuckles turned white.

Nettie felt so lonely she couldn't stop the tears that had been building up all day. She reached into the pillowcase, where she had hidden her mother's dictionary, then pressed her face into the pillow to stifle the sobs. When they finally stopped, she got up and walked to the window, inched it up, and leaned out into the cold night air. She had never been up so high. Back in Jasper, every house they'd ever lived in had only one floor. No matter how cramped the inside was, each room, by door or window, led outside.

Nettie remembered other times when she couldn't sleep, how she'd go out and count the stars until she was so tired, she could barely find her way back to bed. Here, she could see only a tiny bit of sky. No stars. No moon.

Everything was different. And yet everything would be the same. They would stay awhile, and then it would happen. One of them would need new shoes or a winter coat. Or maybe one of them would get sick and have to go to a doctor, and back they'd go again to Grandma Bessie.

Nettie was tired, but not tired enough to sleep. The windowsill was wide, wide enough to sit on, so she climbed up and rested her head against the moist, cool glass. She looked for the lady in the window, but her window was dark and empty. One by one, all along the street, lights went off. Nettie began to count.

Nettie couldn't remember closing the window and getting into bed. She lay there wondering how she had when she heard the grandfather's voice. She looked across the hall. John Peter was still asleep. She crept out of bed and went to the doorway.

The grandfather was standing at the entrance to his bedroom. "Did you sleep well, Cassie?" He hugged the cat to him. "I slept better than I have slept in a long time."

Nettie turned quickly, hoping the grandfather hadn't seen her, but as soon as she got back into bed, he appeared in the doorway.

"Good morning, Natasha. May we come in?"

Nettie hesitated, then nodded. No one had ever asked her permission to come into a room, not even her and John Peter's room at Grandma Bessie's.

The grandfather settled himself on the edge of the bed,

the cat tucked under his arm. "I thought today we could take a long walk —"

Cassie leapt down from his arms, walked over to the door, and meowed.

"I know. You want breakfast. Be patient."

The grandfather turned back to Nettie. "It will be good for you children to get acquainted with the neighborhood. Perhaps go by the school you will go to." He shrugged. "I would have liked to send you both to St. Leonard's. Your father went there." He sighed. "For now it is too costly. But," he said, raising his finger, shaking it back and forth, "when my business gets busy again, things will be better for all of us." He looked over at Cassie. "Right, my friend?"

Wrong, thought Nettie. Wrong. Wrong. Wrong.

He stood up. "Now it is time I get breakfast for Cassie and the rest of us."

Nettie had forgotten all about school. Thinking about it sent a shiver down her back. She'd always loved school, but she had read enough to know that schools in Boston were different than those in Jasper. More teachers. More students. More of everything to get used to. Nettie didn't make friends easily. It took her time to find somebody who she could get close to, and moving around the way they did, it seemed as soon as she found a friend, they'd be off again. Being back at Grandma Bessie's didn't help either. "Don't want kids comin' and goin'," she'd always say. "First thing you know, the whole town'll know my business."

John Peter would do more than shiver at the thought of school. He'd stutter more than ever. His stuttering got worse when he had to go into a new school with kids he didn't know. And it was awful when kids poked fun at him. Sometimes he'd stutter so bad, he'd have trouble getting his breath.

The smell of coffee and toast filled Nettie's nostrils. She wondered if the grandfather would burn that, too. She also got to wondering why Grandma Bessie had never mentioned that they had an aunt named Aleta and why the grandfather had to look after her.

John Peter appeared in the doorway, rubbing his eyes. "How come you never sang me a story? I waited and you never came." She was just about to tell him how he pushed her away, how he wouldn't let her help him, how he'd let the grandfather undress him. But again he said, "I waited, Nettie, and you never came."

The lonely feeling lifted. "I guess I was too tired," Nettie said, her voice soft and gentle. "Come on, I'll tell you one now." She threw back the covers. "Only I can't sing it. Remember what Grandma Bessie said."

"Even if we hide under the covers?" John Peter said, climbing in beside her.

She threw the covers over their heads and began to sing softly. "One day we left Jasper and boarded a train, it took us to Boston —"

John Peter joined in. "And then back again —"

Nettie shook her head. "Oh, no, not to Jasper —"

"AHHH." The grandfather's voice bounced down the

hallway, and the smell of something burning seeped under the covers.

Nettie threw the covers off and leapt out of bed, ran down the hall, and into the kitchen.

"I like my toast well done, Natasha," he said, scraping a piece of burnt toast. "How about you?"

⇥ CHAPTER NINE ⇤

The grandfather poured orange juice into Nettie's and John Peter's glasses, filled their bowls with huge globs of oatmeal, spooned some into Cassie's dish, and finally dropped the last of it into his.

"Did you sleep well, Natasha?" the grandfather asked, putting the oatmeal pot into the sink, motioning for them to sit down.

"Yes, thank you."

"And you, J.P. How did you sleep?"

"F-f-fine, th-thank you."

The grandfather sat down, tucked his napkin under his chin, and ruffled John Peter's hair. "You sound very much like your father when he was your age."

"H-he st-tuttered?"

The grandfather nodded. "Only when he rushed his words."

This was too much for Nettie. "I never heard him stutter," she said. "Ever."

"I would be surprised if you had. The older he got, the less he rushed." He looked back at John Peter. "Take your time. Time takes care of all life's problems." He took a deep breath, glanced up, and shook his head. "Not all." Then, looking back at John Peter, he said, "But time will take care of yours, my boy."

"I . . . slept . . . good."

"Fine," Nettie corrected.

"F-fine." John Peter was smiling as though his stuttering was solved forever, when the grandfather was probably saying their father stuttered to make them think he was an expert on everything.

"Let us eat now," the grandfather said, bowing his head and saying a quick prayer before putting a big spoon of oatmeal into his mouth. He swallowed hard, his eyes opening wide. *"Terribile. Molto terribile."* He dropped his spoon. "The worst." Glancing down at Cassie, he said, "Even Cassie knows how awful it is. She refuses to eat it." He looked back at Nettie and John Peter. "And so should you."

It was more than awful. It was disgusting, but at Grandma Bessie's table, Nettie and John Peter ate whatever was put in front of them. Same way with Cousin Jen and all the rest. It was sinful to waste food.

John Peter put his spoon down. Nettie kicked him under the table. "We don't waste food." John Peter picked up his spoon.

"I am not one to be wasteful, Natasha, but when my cat refuses to eat something, I think it only right that my guests do likewise."

John Peter put his spoon down again. "I'm not eating it. Pa says I don't have to."

"Please excuse us," Nettie said. She took John Peter's arm and yanked him into the hall.

"You're eating it whether you like it or not."

"Why?"

"Because that's what we've always done, and things are no different here. You eat what's in front of you, same as always."

"But Pa said —"

"Did you hear what else he said? He called us guests. That's what we always are. Guests. And do guests stay forever?"

"But Nett —"

"Don't but-Nettie me —"

"You sound just like Grandma Bessie. 'Don't go Grandma-Bessieing me,'" he mimicked. "And you're acting meaner than her —"

"Than she," Nettie said, pushing him in the direction of the kitchen. "And mean or not," she hissed, "I'm in charge, so eat your breakfast."

After breakfast, true to what Nettie had promised herself, she cleared up the kitchen while John Peter and the grandfather dressed. She scrubbed the oatmeal pot and was surprised that hot water came right from the spigot. Water was always heated on the stove in Jasper. It felt good to put her hands under the warm water, warm until the final dish was washed and rinsed.

Nettie was just about to wipe the table down when the grandfather came into the kitchen. "See how fast she works, Cassie. Like her grandmother." He took the sponge from Nettie's hand. "Let me finish. You go and dress. Today is special."

He smiled his lopsided smile. "Today we play. Two, three days is time enough to register at school."

That's all they seemed to do. Register for school. It wasn't even the middle of February, and this would be their third school since the beginning of the winter term.

"Do you like school, Natasha?" he asked, rubbing a spot on the table.

"I liked them in Jasper."

"What about J.P.? Excuse me, John Peter," he said, tossing the sponge into the sink. "Just now he told me that is what he prefers to be called."

Nettie was amazed. Shocked. John Peter always depended on her to do things like that. "Tell Grandma Bessie I don't want any more peas," he'd say, or "Tell Miss Onthank I was sick and couldn't do my homework —"

"Natasha?"

"Excuse me?"

"Does John Peter like school?"

"Sometimes."

"Like your father. He did well in what he liked. Ahh, but arithmetic! Did you know how he hated that?"

Nettie stiffened. She wasn't going to be trapped again the way she always had been. Talking about Poppa. And Momma. Cousin Jen or whoever they were staying with would say one little thing about them, and Nettie would want to know more. Beg to know more.

58

"John Peter looks like him, too. Do you agree?"

"I suppose."

"Did you see his photograph?"

"No."

"Come."

Nettie followed him into the hall, reminding herself that it was just a picture taken a long time ago.

The grandfather carefully took the picture from its place, rubbed the glass on his sleeve, and placed it in Nettie's hands. He cleared his throat. "He was nine years old."

Nettie's throat tightened. *He is like John Peter.* Looking at the picture, she was back at Morgan Creek, her father lifting John Peter to his shoulders, her mother calling —

"Would you like to have it?"

Nettie hesitated, wanting it, but only for the time it took her to remember the day Rose Ellen gave her a picture of her mother. "You may not look like your mother," Rose Ellen had said, "but you surely do act like her. All sweet and nice."

Nettie had placed her mother's picture on the table beside her bed, where she could look at it before she went to sleep and when she woke up. But before the day was over, she and John Peter were bouncing around in the back of Rose Ellen's car, heading on back to Grandma Bessie, the picture back at Cousin Rose Ellen's.

"No, thank you," Nettie said. She carefully hung the picture back on its hook. "It belongs here."

"Are you sure?"

Nettie nodded.

"Should you change your mind, it will be here for you."

He was about to say something else, but the cat appeared from nowhere and wrapped herself around his legs, meowing. "Ahh, you heard we are going out and you want to come. You are too old. If you got lost you might not be able to find your way home." He leaned over and rubbed Cassie's back. "I would miss you." Looking back up at Nettie, he asked, "Do you know how old she is?"

"Five?"

"My granddaughter flatters you." He picked up the cat and pulled gently on her ear. "She is ninety-four cat years old." He looked at the cat for a long minute, rubbing her all the while. "But ninety-four years is still not enough time." He looked up. "Not nearly enough."

He smiled his odd smile. "Now come, Natasha," he said, putting the cat down, "get your brother. It is time we start our day."

"The ocean. Where is it? Nettie said we could jump in the water from your house. Can we go?" John Peter babbled all the way down the stairs. The grandfather and Nettie followed.

"And Nettie wants to see Louisburg Square. And Isabella's garden. Don't you, Nettie?"

"He calls you Nettie," the grandfather said. "Would you prefer I do also?"

"It doesn't matter." For whatever time they would be here, it didn't matter.

He smiled. "Good. I shall call you Natasha."

When John Peter got to the last step, instead of going outside, he turned toward the door to the funeral parlor. Looking back at the grandfather, he asked if he could go in.

"There really is not much to see. An organ. Old silk flowers. Some dust. But if you want, go in." He turned to Nettie. "And you, too."

She shook her head and watched John Peter open the door and walk through as though he was going through any ordinary doorway. She listened as he asked the grandfather what the viewing room was, and what was kept in the showroom, and if there were bodies where would they be. Her breath came fast as she listened to the grandfather tell him the viewing room was where families gathered to pay their respects to the dead, and the showroom was where the coffins were stored. But she blocked out the answer to where the bodies were kept and didn't hear any more until she heard the grandfather say, "Enough, John Peter. Come. There is more to see on the outside of DeAngelus and Son than on the inside."

⇥ Chapter Ten ⇤

The air was frigid, the sky a dismal gray. Nettie felt anxious, her head in tomorrow and the next day and the next. Living with Uncle Ben was the only time Nettie stopped worrying about everything. He wouldn't let her. "Kee-rist, girl, stop puttin' the worries of the world on those skinny little shoulders. I'm tellin' you, you're gonna get cockeyed with one eye on yesterday and the other on tomorrow." Then he'd cross his eyes and Nettie would laugh. "Enjoy the day, girl. It's all we got."

Grandma Bessie always said that's what did him in. Enjoying the day. "A man his age flyin' around on those rafters. Daft. That's what he is."

Nettie sighed a very long sigh and thrust her hands into her pockets and told John Peter to put on his hat. "Do you want an earache?"

Without answering, John Peter yanked his hat out of his coat sleeve, pulled it down over his ears, and took the grandfather's arm. Watching him, Nettie felt angry.

62

Wait. Just wait. When we're leaving, you won't be skipping. And it won't be his arm you're clinging to —

"*Buon giorno,* Frank," the man standing in the doorway of the butcher shop called. "Nice to see you." He turned the "Closed" sign to "Open." "These are John's children?"

The grandfather nodded and smiled his tight smile. "Yes. Yes. Natasha and John Peter."

The man stepped down from his shop, took Nettie's hand in his and lightly kissed it. "My pleasure." Nettie had only read about people doing that. Her face flushed with embarrassment. "You are your grandmother's child." He turned to John Peter. "Ahh, but you. You have the face of your father."

Passing the barbershop, the grandfather peered in the window, and when the barber saw him, he stopped cutting his customer's hair and came to the door, waving his scissors. "So you are out of hibernation, Francesco." He pinched John Peter's cheek. "I would know John's baby anywhere. *Bello.*" Still holding his scissors, he clasped his hands together. "And you," he said to Nettie, "*molto bella.*"

"I'm no baby," John Peter said as soon as the door closed behind the barber. "And what else did he call me?"

"He said you were beautiful," the grandfather said. "And that Natasha was very beautiful."

"Boys aren't beautiful."

The grandfather laughed. "Today everybody and every thing is beautiful. Even this dark, dismal day."

63

"Frank. Frank," a lady called from the door of Vincenzo's Bake Shop, her stockings, like giant Cheerios, rolled down to her ankles. "Are these the grandchildren?"

"Yes. They have come from Ohio."

The lady in the window called down a hello and a how-good-God-is-to-send-the-children-to-visit.

"Yes," the grandfather called back, "He is very good."

Visiting. That's what we always do. Visit.

The grandfather guided them down the narrow sidewalk, made narrower by the tires of cars and trucks parked on the curb. The grandfather talked on, showing them where the best cappuccino and sweets were made. Where the finest pizza could be had.

"The ocean, Pa," John Peter whined. "I want to see the ocean."

"The harbor. It is only a harbor."

"But I want to see it. Now. Please."

Coming to a church, the grandfather announced this was their first stop. "Everyone must see this," he said. Nettie knew from her reading it was the Old North Church. She wanted to see it, badly, but John Peter carried on about the ocean and why couldn't they see it now. "Please, Nettie? Please?"

Nettie gave up and the grandfather ushered them across the street and up a hill. At the top, he pointed to what he told them was the narrowest house in all of Boston. But John Peter was more interested in what was at the bottom of the hill. The ocean. And Nettie was more than interested in what was beside them — "Copp's Hill Burying Ground," the sign read. From where Nettie stood, she could see nothing beyond the rows and rows of headstones. It was as though the rest of the earth had fallen away.

"Nettie, come on," John Peter shouted, climbing the stairs into the burial ground. "Pa says we can see the ocean better if we walk through here."

Nothing could make Nettie walk through a cemetery. It was bad enough to be staying in a funeral home, she didn't have to tramp through a cemetery, too.

"Do you think I can go back to the church?" she asked the grandfather.

"We will not be long."

"I'm cold."

The grandfather hestitated, then nodded. "Be sure to wait for us in the front of the church. And do not speak to anyone."

At the church a crowd had gathered, and Nettie found herself swept along as they entered the front door. She stopped to listen to an old man tell the history of the church. How on the night of April 18, 1775, the young sexton had climbed the steeple to hang the two lanterns that would begin Paul Revere's ride. How twice the steeple had toppled during hurricanes. How the worshipers brought their own little coal stoves to keep their feet warm. Nettie was enjoying it all until the lecturer told them they were standing on hallowed ground. "There are almost one thousand bodies buried where we stand. Unknown seamen from other nations and famous men from —"

Nettie blocked out the rest and looked around her. Everything was white. Walls and pews. Ceilings and columns. Chandeliers glistened, and the clear glass windows allowed light to come through. Grandma Bessie's church was small and shadowy, its windows covered with heavy dark draperies that blocked out even the sunniest day. Nettie hated going there, hated listening to the Reverend Claypoole talk about the evils of sin. How the devil walked among them, ready to take possession of somebody's soul. "A thief is among us," he shouted one bleak Sunday morning. "Behind you. Beside you. In front of you. He's everywhere. The only escape is to cleanse yourselves."

Nettie remembered how John Peter's head swiveled around, how he refused to get out of the bathtub that night, how he crept into Nettie's bed long after Grandma Bessie slept.

"— that concludes our little tour of Old North Church. You are most welcome to visit the Washington Memorial Garden and the Paul Revere Mall. Or if you prefer, browse in our gift shop."

The crowd moved out to the gift shop and Nettie moved along with them. She wasn't there long when she heard the grandfather's voice. "Has anybody seen a young girl —"

The grandfather, his voice stern, told Nettie how concerned he'd been when she wasn't where he'd told her to wait.

"I am responsible for you. What would I tell your grandmother if something happened to you?"

"I can take care of myself," Nettie said. "Grandma Bessie wouldn't care. She never worried."

"I am not Grandma Bessie and I worry. While you are with me, you will please do as I ask." He forced a small smile.

Since Nettie had seen the church and John Peter wasn't interested, it was decided they would take a train into downtown Boston.

At the subway station, while the grandfather made change and bought tokens, John Peter whispered into Nettie's ear. "You should have waited where he told you. He was worried."

"He was more worried about what he'd tell Grandma Bessie."

"Come, children," the grandfather said, depositing the tokens for them. "First to the Public Gardens —"

John Peter pushed his way through the turnstile. "Pa says he's going to show you Louisburg Square."

"It's Lou-is-burg, not Loo-ee-burg —"

"But Pa said —"

"It's Lou-is-burg," Nettie said, reaching for John Peter's hand. But John Peter shook it off, took the grandfather's hand, and, in a loud whisper, said, "I like the way Pa says it better."

⌐ CHAPTER ELEVEN ⌐

They never did get to Louisburg Square or the Public Gardens. As soon as they left the subway, it began to rain. They stood under a store awning for a while, hoping the rain would stop. It didn't, and when John Peter began to sneeze, the grandfather said it was time they went back. "You have been sneezing off and on since you arrived," the grandfather said. "Perhaps you are catching cold."

Nettie told him John Peter sometimes did that.

"Grandma Bessie always told me I did it to grind up her nerves," John Peter said.

But it didn't get on the grandfather's nerves. He wrapped his jacket around John Peter, and when he began to shiver, the grandfather stood in the rain, waving his arms at every passing taxi. One finally pulled over to the curb, and they piled into the backseat.

The grandfather fussed over John Peter and, once back at the apartment, insisted John Peter get into bed. He made him hot soup and got him extra pillows. Took his temperature. Felt his forehead. And every time he sneezed or sniffled, the grandfather was beside him.

"How do you feel?"

"Does your head hurt?"

"Cover up now."

The grandfather checked John Peter's temperature a thousand times and sat with him until he fell asleep. John Peter enjoyed every minute of it, but as Nettie watched from across the hall, an empty feeling washed over her.

She lay back and stared at the ceiling, then closed her eyes and let sleep come.

"Aaaachoo! Aaaachoo!"

Nettie sat up in bed and rubbed her eyes, not knowing where she was until she saw the light coming from the street lamp outside the window.

"Aaaachoo!"

It was John Peter again. Nettie put her head under the pillow, hoping he'd go back to sleep. But he didn't and just as Nettie was getting ready to go into him, she heard the grandfather's footsteps.

She got out of bed and watched as the grandfather rested his hand on John Peter's forehead. "You have no fever," he said, tucking the covers around John Peter. "I cannot understand this —"

Again John Peter sneezed.

"Ahh! Where has my head been?"

Nettie watched as the grandfather picked up Cassie

from the foot of the bed. "You are the problem." He tucked the cat under his arm. "What do you think of that?"

John Peter sneezed his answer.

"No more sleeping with your new friend," the grandfather said, walking back to his room with Cassie. "You will have to make do with your old one." He called back a good-night to John Peter. "Sleep well. You also, Natasha."

Nettie crawled back into bed and pulled the covers around her. The light from the outside street lamp lit up the bare floor.

A sneeze and then Nettie felt John Peter's hand on her shoulder.

"Nettie," he whispered, "I'm scared."

The empty feeling left. Nettie reached out to him. "Of what?" she asked.

"Pa says I'm allergic to Cassie."

"So?"

"If I'm allergic, probably one of us will have to leave." He sneezed again. "Can I get in bed with you? Just for a while?"

Nettie lifted the covers and he snuggled in.

"Pa loves Cassie," he whimpered.

Nettie covered him. "It'll be all right, John Peter. I'm here."

John Peter sobbed a huge sob. "I don't want to go back to Grandma Bessie."

"We're not going back. I told you that. I'll think of something."

"But Cassie's been here a long time and I've only been here for two days."

"What's that to do with anything?"

"If one of us has to go, it'll be me."

"Maybe we can get some of those pills for allergic people."

"Can we get them tomorrow?"

"First thing."

He sneezed again. "But they cost money."

"I've got six dollars and eighty cents from Grandma Bessie's money. Don't worry."

"Can I stay with you tonight?" Another sneeze.

"Sure," she said. Pulling the covers up over them, she sang, very softly, "Over the sea to sky —"

Nettie woke with a start, John Peter asleep beside her. She heard the grandfather say something to Cassie and then heard him rummaging around in John Peter's room. Nettie slid out of bed and watched from the door. The grandfather took John Peter's pillow out of its case and examined the tag that hung from the ticking. He turned quickly, too quickly for Nettie to move.

"Good morning, Natasha. I am playing Sherlock Holmes." He gazed up. "Anna, *cara mia,* your feather pillow is the cuprit." Looking back at Nettie, he said, "John Peter sneezed in your bed, too, did he not?"

Without waiting for an answer, he told her how her grandmother had loved feather pillows but could never use them. "She was allergic to goose down. She sneezed the way John Peter does." He stuffed the pillow into a plastic bag. "I think it best if we get rid of your pillow, too." Again he looked up. "I can do without the pillows but not Cassie."

Nettie slipped the pillow out from beneath John Peter's head, placed her mother's dictionary in the drawer of the bedside table, and wondered if anybody would ever say they couldn't do without them.

⊰ CHAPTER TWELVE ⊱

From the kitchen, Nettie heard a woman's high-pitched voice, rising and falling as though keeping time to some silent tune. Then the grandfather, his voice flat, slightly on edge. "The girl is Natasha, the boy John Peter."

Nettie crept down the narrow hallway and listened.

"Why did you keep the day secret? Three days my sister's grandbabies are here —"

Nettie peered into the kitchen. A tall, skinny lady, her spiky heels clicking, her long dark hair bouncing, paced back and forth on the worn linoleum.

"Call them, Frank. I am bursting to see them."

"Time enough when breakfast is ready. The boy still sleeps."

Coming to the doorway leading to the hall, the woman stopped. "Oh. My. God. You must be Natasha." She wrapped her arms around Nettie, looked up, and closed her eyes. For a minute Nettie thought she was going to talk to Anna, too, but she didn't. Eyes still closed, she took Nettie's face in her hands. "I have been waiting for this moment for years. Years of hoping Bessie would come to her senses and send you where you rightfully belong. Years of waiting. Longing. Yearning."

From the kitchen, Nettie heard a loud groan.

"Yes, Frank, I said yearning." She looked down at Nettie, tears ready to spill. "For once Frank and I agree. You are so very much like my dear sister." She smoothed Nettie's hair. "I'm your aunt Aleta. Come, let's get your brother."

She swept Nettie down the hallway and into where John Peter slept. Again, she looked up. Again, she said how long she'd waited for this day. Yearned for this day. And, again, tears waited to spill from her eyes.

John Peter sat up in bed and clutched the covers to his chest.

Aleta cupped his chin in her hand. "The face of an angel. So like our John." She kissed his cheek.

John Peter flinched. Aleta kissed his other cheek. "I'm Aleta, your aunt, dear sweet boy."

John Peter looked at Nettie and rolled his eyes. But Nettie was enjoying it all. Aleta intrigued her. She was the most elegant person Nettie had ever seen. Even with a nose that was much too large for her face, there was something very beautiful about her. She had the longest fingers Nettie had ever seen. And her nails. They were almost as long as her fingers. They were painted dark red and had tiny, luminous stars embedded in the middle of each one. Her lashes were black and curled up all the way to her eyebrows. Her skin was the color of parchment stretched taut. She wore a long black silky skirt; a short crimson cape covered her shoulders. And she smelled so good.

"Well, now," Aleta said, taking Nettie's hand, reaching down for John Peter's, "Frank tells me he walked you round the neighborhood, showed you the harbor, and walked you through the burial ground." She lowered her voice to a whisper. "That's just like him. Bo-oorr-ring, I say. And you probably froze your tootsies off. Right?"

John Peter said nothing. Nettie shrugged.

"Well, there are lots better things to do and we are going to do them all.

"There are shops and movies and fun places to eat. And come summer we'll go to Revere Beach. How about that?

"And we'll do the swan boats come spring." She clasped her hands together. "The Freedom Trail. All sorts of things."

Nettie was about to ask about Mrs. Gardner's museum, but the grandfather appeared in the doorway.

"Good morning, John Peter. You slept without sneezing."

John Peter smiled his answer.

"Sneezing? He probably caught his death of cold parading around the neighborhood. You do the touring thing in May or June, not in February."

"He has not caught cold. It is an allergy and the cause has been found. Anna's pillows. Now come," he said, heading back toward the kitchen, "breakfast is ready, and you are welcome to join us."

"I expected to. After all, I am their aunt. Their one and only." She smiled at John Peter. "On your father's side, that is. Now come, sweet child, time to get up."

"I-I-I c-c-can't. I-I-I'm n-n-not dressed."

"Does he always do that, Natasha?"

"Excuse me?"

"Stutter."

"Just when he's upset."

"Well, there's nothing for him to be upset about." Aleta bent down and gave him another kiss. "Nothing at all. We're family, aren't we?" She kissed him again. "One big, happy family." Taking John Peter's hand, putting her arm around Natasha, she said, "Well, maybe not so very big, but we're going to be happy. Yes, we are."

All during breakfast, Aleta chatted away about how Nettie could spend some time at her place. "Girl stuff. Sleepovers," she said. How they could talk far into the night. "Won't that be fun?" And how John Peter and the grandfather could go to ball games and do boy stuff. She leaned over toward John Peter. "Don't wear him out, though."

The grandfather said little, but every once in a while a shake of his head spoke for him. Almost like Nettie did when John Peter was doing something she didn't like. He was her brother and she cared about him. They were family, just like Aleta had said.

Thinking about all the other things that Aleta had said, Nettie allowed herself to think that maybe, just maybe, there *was* a way for them to stay.

ᴴ⚹ CHAPTER THIRTEEN ⚹ᴴ

"Well, now," Aleta said after breakfast was over, "how about we do something exciting this morning. It will be our first adventure."

"I planned to take the children by the school this morning."

"That is not fair, Frank. First you keep their arrival a secret —"

"I told you earlier, I did not keep —"

"— and now you whisk them off to school, making it impossible for us to get acquainted —"

"Aleta —"

"— Anna wouldn't like that. She wouldn't like that at all. You know how —"

The grandfather looked up, shook his head, and said, "Impossible. When she gets something into her head, she is impossible."

Aleta paid no attention to him. "— she would want me to be a part of them." She picked up her coffee and drained the cup.

"By the way, what school are they going to?"

"Grove Street."

"With their standards? Why not St. Leonard's? Or something on the Hill?"

The grandfather got up and put his plate in the sink. "St. Leonard's is too costly. Grove Street's standards are fine and it is in my district."

"That's the problem. You're comparing it with schools in your district. Send them out of the district. You can give my address and send them to the one near the Square —"

Nettie felt a rush of excitement surge through her. "Do you live in Louisburg Square?"

"Did you hear that, Frank? The child said Louisburg properly." Aleta gave Nettie a big smile. "People — and they shall be nameless — who have lived in the area for years don't pronounce it correctly."

"So I am nameless," the grandfather said, winking at John Peter.

"If the shoe fits," Aleta said, picking up her plate and putting it in the sink. "I have a great idea, children. Since your grandfather is so fired up about taking you by the school, I'll come along. Then we can go up to the Hill and you can have a look-see at the schools up there. How's that?

"And, Frank, I know the most divine place for lunch. La Petite Dominique." She sat down beside Nettie. "Your grandfather's feet will probably give out after lunch and I know how little guys hate to shop, but we ladies could do some. There are the most glorious shops near the Gardens. We could browse. Maybe have high tea at the Ritz. Would you like that, Natasha?"

Before Nettie could answer, a loud beeping noise, like the sound of an ambulance or a police car, filled the kitchen.

Cassie leapt from the windowsill and slid under the table.

"Don't get excited," Aleta said, reaching under her cape. "It's only my telephone."

Nettie's eyes opened wide; she wasn't sure she was seeing what she thought she saw. John Peter's mouth hung open.

The grandfather looked up and shook his head. "Such a waste, Anna. Such an affectation."

Aleta waved her hand at him and mouthed, "Be still.

"Yes, this is Aleta Bianca.

"What's that? Hannah Macklin. Mmmnn, yes, I think so. Isn't she one of the producers of *Broken Vessels?*

"Today? At what time?" She smiled.

"Let me check my schedule." Putting her hand over the receiver, a pout replacing the smile, she whispered, "I'm sorry. I really am, but I've been waiting for this for forever. Tomorrow. We'll do it all tomorrow." She took her hand off the receiver and said, "I'm on my way to an audition now, but I guess I could be there by four. How would that be?" The smile came back.

"I'd better take your number," Aleta said, the smile getting bigger. "Yes, I have pen in hand.

"I've got it down," Aleta said in her singsong voice. "Ta ta." She breathed in deeply and put the telephone back under her cape. "I can't believe this. I simply can't believe it. Hannah Macklin calling me. Me! Well, not Hannah herself, but one of her staff." She looked over at the grandfather. "Do you know who she is?" She didn't wait for an answer. "Just the best producer of off-Broadway plays on the East Coast. No, I take that back. The best in the country. Do you know what her call means?"

Again, before he could answer she spoke. "She must have a part for me. A part! Do you know how long it's been since I've had a call like that? It has to be two years. Yes, it is two years. It was the year your business went bad."

"I remember, Aleta. I remember very well." The grandfather's voice was as somber as his face.

"Don't start that again," she said, whipping out the telephone. This time she dialed.

"Sarkus? Is that you?

"You did it, my darling. Hannah Macklin finally called. I need you to pick me up.

"Yes, I said Hannah Macklin.

"I'm at Frank's. Okay? Two minutes? Fine." She put the phone back.

"What has Sarkus got to do with all this?" the grandfather asked.

"He's my agent."

"Agent? What can a tailor know about things like this?"

It was as though the grandfather hadn't spoken. "I'm sorry, Natasha. I really am. You, too, John Peter. But this

80

could be my big break." She ran her hand through her hair. "I've got to fix this mess and do my nails and decide what to wear all before four o'clock. But tomorrow we'll do lunch and shop and all those good things."

She gave John Peter a kiss and hugged Nettie hard. "Walk me downstairs, lovey."

Nettie had a million questions she wanted to ask Aleta, but as soon as they got downstairs, a pale pink truck with SARKUS, YOUR FRIENDLY TAILOR blazoned across it pulled up across the street. "Come on, Allie, old girl," the wild-haired driver called out. "Sarkus is at your service."

Giving Nettie a last hug, Aleta clicked across the street, turned back, waved, and blew kisses. "Tomorrow, Natasha. I'll call you first thing tomorrow."

And Nettie called back, "I'll be waiting."

Nettie waved as the pink truck roared down the street, and when it turned the corner and disappeared out of sight, she turned and started up the stairs.

Imagine having an actress for an aunt. An aunt who carries a telephone around with her. An aunt who can call somebody and have that somebody arrive in a pink truck and whisk her away. She must live in a house as beautiful as the ones in the book Miss Hinton gave me. Probably as beautiful as Isabella Stewart Gardner's. Nettie sighed a long, long sigh. *Tomorrow I'll ask her to show me her house. Yes, tomorrow, after lunch at La Petite Dominique, and browsing in Louisburg Square, and drinking high tea, I'll ask her just that.*

⊰ CHAPTER FOURTEEN ⊱

The tomorrow Aleta was to call came, as did six other tomorrows. Every time the phone rang, Nettie's hopes soared. Each time, the grandfather told her to try not to be disappointed, that Aleta meant well but at times got so busy she had trouble keeping promises in the time she promised to keep them. "But one day, she will call."

And she did. The day they were to register for school.

"Hello, Natasha," Aleta said, sounding as though she'd just run a hundred miles. "I'm sorry I haven't called but things got so hectic. Can you forgive your aunt Aleta?"

Of course Nettie could forgive her. "We're registering at Grove Street today," Nettie said, expecting Aleta to say something about the other schools.

"Wonderful. You'll make some friends."

Nettie was good at hiding disappointment. "Did you get the part?"

"Oh, Hannah Macklin wanted me, all right —"

"That's good, isn't it?"

"No, it's not good. She wanted me to do makeup."

"And you didn't want to?"

"I'm through with that. I'm thirty-eight years old and I haven't spent the last umpteen years studying acting to make other people look good onstage. That's where I should be, for God's sake. I'm through with makeup. Well, almost —" Then in a voice as shrill as Grandma Bessie had ever used, "For God's sake, woman, I'll do your mascara in two secs. Keep your shoes on.

"Listen, sweetheart, I've got a lot of antsy ladies in the shop. How about we do some fun things next week? La Petite Dominique, the Ritz. Whatever you want. Okay with you?"

Of course it was okay with Nettie.

"I've got to go now. I'll call you at the end of the week."

"Promise?"

"Of course I promise, but let me give you my number just in case you want to call me. Have you got a pencil?"

Nettie had one.

"Call you Friday, Natasha. Maybe you can sleep over. Love you."

Nettie leaned back and sighed a contented sigh, so sure of Aleta's promise. Next week for sure. She imagined herself in La Petite Dominique ordering from an elegant menu. Browsing in little shops. Having high tea. Imagined herself in Aleta's home, her feet tapping lightly on black marble floors. Walking into a parlor filled with ornately carved furniture, her feet sinking into the carpet, plopping herself on a silky red sofa.

Wandering upstairs and into the bedrooms, one more beautiful than the other. Puffs and pillows piled high on beds big enough to sleep three people. Ruffly curtains at each window. Bottles and bottles of expensive perfume on dressers and on bathroom vanities.

Nettie brushed aside the disappointment of Aleta's not remembering about the schools on the Hill. Put aside her promise to herself of not being too hopeful, because surely somebody who had been waiting years for them to arrive, somebody who said, "We're family, aren't we?", somebody who had money to go to fancy restaurants for lunch and high tea, somebody who dressed like a queen and carried her own telephone, would help them stay —

"Natasha," the grandfather's voice called from the kitchen, "come get your breakfast. Our appointment is in less than an hour."

They were to be tested at school that day. Nettie hated that. So did John Peter. But Grandma Bessie hadn't sent their records, and the principal said that in addition to being inoculated, academic testing was mandatory. "We all have various aptitudes, gifts, as it were," Mrs. Fiorey said, "and it's my job to see that these gifts are nourished. The tests will do that."

The grandfather piled eggs on their plates, poured juice and milk in tumblers, then went to get dressed. John Peter devoured his eggs, gulped down his milk and juice, and announced he had a bad stomachache. "I think I'm having an allergy to the shots the doctor gave us. I'd better wait to take the tests." Nettie knew he was faking, but she was anxious about the day, too. She put her hand on his and told him that he'd better go back to bed. "It's not really an allergy, just an allergic reaction. Maybe we better wait until tomorrow."

Coming back into the kitchen, the grandfather said, "No, Natasha, we will go today. Tomorrow is always the day we are certain we will face without fear. That thinking is false and to learn it at an early age is good. Now come, it is time we start."

The school was a tall, ugly yellow brick building set in the middle of a cement yard surrounded by a high fence. All the schools that Nettie had gone to in Ohio were small, one-story buildings, with lots of tall grass around them, and usually from one of the trees a swing hung; bicycles were propped against trees, or against the building, or left lying in the grass. But the Grove Street Elementary School had no grass. No trees. No bicycles. And the swings hung from rusty metal posts. It loomed before Nettie and looked more like a prison than a school.

Mrs. Fiorey was waiting for them at the door of her office. "You're very welcome to wait here, Mr. De-Angelus," she said, "but if you have business to get on with, Natasha and John Peter should be finished in about two hours."

"W-wait here," John Peter said. "Please."

John Peter spoke slowly, deliberately, all the while

looking up at the grandfather. John Peter was getting so attached to him. He rarely poked Nettie to whisper in her ear what he wanted to say, especially when the grandfather was around. It surprised Nettie that she missed it so much.

A hand on her shoulder broke into her thoughts. "Come along, Natasha," Mrs. Fiorey said, "I'll take you to Mr. Caputo. He's waiting for you." She turned to John Peter. "You'll be testing with Mrs. Peterson."

"*Buona fortuna,* Natasha," the grandfather said. "Good luck."

Nettie smiled a tiny smile and followed Mrs. Fiorey down the long, gray corridor. March music blared from one of the rooms. "That's our marching band." She guided Nettie over to a large, sun-filled room. "This is a new group." She smiled. "Sounds pretty awful but by June, they'll sound better."

"Jeanne," a voice called, "I'm setting up in here."

"Be there in a minute, Peter," Mrs. Fiorey called back. "Remember, Natasha," she went on, "Mr. Caputo is testing you to determine where your strengths are. Relax and enjoy the process. It's painless, I assure you."

And it was.

After Nettie completed each segment, Mr. Caputo went over it. English. Math. Science. And last, an essay on what she most enjoyed learning about. When he finished reading it, he asked if she had been in an enrichment program at her last school.

"No. They didn't have one."

"You must have been in a music program."

"I sang in the chorus for a while."

"For a while? The way you write about it I would think nothing would stop you. Why did you?"

Nettie was too embarrassed to admit that Grandma Bessie said it was a waste of time, so she told him it had interfered with her schoolwork.

He gave her a puzzled look. "Hmmmnn. Hard to imagine anything interfering with *your* schoolwork. Tell me, are you a soprano? Alto?"

"Soprano."

"Great. My chorus can use a good one." He instructed Nettie to gather up her belongings. "Is one of your parents here with you?"

"My grandfather."

"I'd like to meet him."

When they turned into the principal's office and the grandfather came to shake Mr. Caputo's hand, Mr. Caputo smiled and said, "I should have known as soon as I saw the name."

He turned to Nettie. "You come by it naturally." Then back to the grandfather. "Where have you been keeping yourself?"

The grandfather shrugged. "With Anna gone, the business gone — what can I say? I have become a hermit." He glanced over at Nettie. "Until last week."

"They still haven't gotten anybody down at church who can come near what you made that old organ do. Ever think of coming back?"

The grandfather shook his head. "My desire to play died with Anna."

"Maybe in time." He shook the grandfather's hand, excused himself, and went into Mrs. Fiorey's office.

The grandfather looked over at Nettie. "This does not surprise me. I heard you singing to John Peter —"

"I'm sorry. I didn't mean to —"

"Sorry? To sing is nothing you should feel sorry about." He patted the space on the bench next to him. "Come, Natasha, sit down. There's something I want to ask you before John Peter gets back."

An uneasy feeling took hold of her. Whenever John Peter wasn't to hear something, it was usually bad news. But when she sat at the end of the bench, all he asked her was did she think he had been too hard on John Peter. "He was very upset when the teacher took him to be tested. Do you think he is really not feeling well?"

Before she could answer, the door opened and John Peter burst through. The woman with him introduced herself to the grandfather. "It's so nice to know you, Mr. DeAngelus. John has been telling me so much about you." She turned to Nettie. "And you must be Natasha." She smiled. "Well, now, after testing John, third grade is exactly where he should be —"

"That's what I told Mrs. Fiorey," Nettie said. "And I should be in sixth —"

"Seventh, Natasha," Mrs. Fiorey said as she came into the outer office. "Mr. Caputo thinks you're too advanced for sixth."

"But I did fine in sixth grade."

"And you'll do fine in seventh." Turning to her secretary, she said, "John Peter is to go into Mr. Stein's class, Natasha in Miss Cottrell's."

John Peter waved a weak good-bye to the grandfather. Nettie took John Peter's hand and realized that, for the first time in her entire life, it was to give herself comfort, not John Peter.

"Pa said he'll meet us after school," he whispered when the secretary pointed to the room assigned to him. "By the front door, Nettie. Right?"

"Right," Nettie said, squeezing his hand. "By the front door." Then she took a deep breath and waved a weaker good-bye to John Peter than he'd waved to the grandfather.

⊰ Chapter Fifteen ⊱

"May I have your attention, boys and girls," Miss Cottrell announced. "We have a new girl. Natasha DeAngelus." She put her hand on Nettie's shoulder. "Please join me in welcoming Natasha to the Grove Street School."

Every pair of eyes was on Nettie, as if she was the first new girl to come to Grove Street in the last century.

"Josephine, would you be kind enough to escort Natasha to the seat directly to your right?"

A tall girl, wearing a dress that was too tight across her chest, made her way to the front of the room. Nettie knew she'd seen her before but couldn't remember where.

Nettie followed her down the fifth aisle to the last seat.

"Thank you, Josephine." Miss Cottrell smiled a tight smile; her long, slightly crooked teeth rested on her bottom lip. "And now, Natasha, would you like to tell the class where you come from? I'm sure they'd all like to know."

Nettie knew that the class didn't really care where she came from. And neither did Miss Cottrell. It was just something teachers did.

"Well?"

"Ohio," Nettie said, biting the inside of her mouth.

"Ohio, how interesting. Cincinnati? Columbus? Just where in Ohio?"

"Jasper."

A wave of stifled laughter washed across the room.

"And what is so funny, class?" Miss Cottrell asked.

"Nothing, Miss Cottrell," the class said in unison.

"Would you like to tell the class where Jasper is, Natasha? Is it in the northern part of the state? Southern?"

"Southwest."

"One day soon, class, on map day, we'll plan an Ohio day, and Nettie can tell us all about Jasper. How does that sound?"

It was always this way. Coming in when the whole class knew one another. Always the new girl with the teacher asking her the same questions. *What is your favorite subject? Did you play sports at your last school?* And then the ones Nettie dreaded most: *Will your parents be coming in for School Night? Or Do you think your mother would like to join the PTA?* And now a new one — *Wherever did you get the name Natasha?"*

And always there was a Josephine to drag Nettie around the first day or two. A Josephine who was either more of a misfit than Nettie or one who was the most popular girl in the class. Either way, Nettie never found a friend.

Miss Cottrell's questions kept coming. "I hear midwesterners speak English much more in keeping with our English ancestors. How do you think we Bostonians measure up?"

Nettie wished the floor would open up and consume her. Or a fire alarm would sound and everybody would evacuate the school. "Well?" Again the tight smile, the long slightly crooked teeth resting on her bottom lip. "We're waiting."

And then the sound of a bell, the sound of books slammed shut, the sound of recess.

"Line up," Miss Cottrell commanded. "Girls to the right. Boys to the left. Josephine, would you be kind enough to guide Natasha through recess?"

"I know you," Josephine whispered the minute Miss Cottrell turned her back. "You live right across the street from me. Four-sixty-one. With Mr. DeAngelus. Right?"

Nettie nodded. She was the girl the lady in the window called to.

"I asked you to guide Natasha, Josephine. And here you are breaking one of the cardinal rules: talking before you get to the cafeteria."

"Sorry, Miss Cottrell."

"Eighth-graders first," the lady at the cafeteria food counter yelled. "Then on down till the fourth gets theirs." Nettie was handed a container of milk and two cookies. She followed Josephine to a table in the corner, surprised to see that the girls sat on one side of the cafeteria, the boys on the other. Nettie searched for John Peter, eager to see how he was doing. She finally spotted him. Two bigger boys sat on each side of him. He had a straw in his mouth and the next thing Nettie knew, its paper wrapper was flying through the air. The boys laughed and so did he.

Nettie got up and headed over to him.

"You can't do that," Josephine said, taking Nettie by the arm. "Girls aren't allowed on the boys' side. Miss Cottrell made up that dumb rule last term."

"I have to see my brother."

"Do you want me to get in real trouble?"

Nettie pulled her arm free and started over.

"Suit yourself. But I'll have to tell Miss Cottrell I tried to stop you or she'll give me a month's detention."

Nettie wanted to say she could tell Miss Cottrell anything she wanted, that she was going to see John Peter. But before Nettie could get to the boys' side, one of the teachers escorted her back.

"I tried to tell you," Josephine said.

Nettie opened her milk and sipped the warm liquid.

"Terrible, huh?" Josephine said. "The milkman comes at seven and we get it at ten. I keep telling my mother I don't want it, but does she listen?"

Nettie was barely listening. She was looking over at John Peter, finding it hard to believe what her eyes saw. He actually looked different since she'd last seen him. Bigger, almost. He was usually the one who took ages to get used to a new school. It was always Nettie who helped him.

Nettie spit some waxy substance from her mouth, her eyes still on John Peter.

"That stuff always comes loose. Miss Cottrell says we have to endure it because of the boys. She says milk is better in glass containers but the boys would end up throwing them at one another. She is Looney Tunes when it comes to boys."

A hollow feeling began in Nettie's chest when the recess-is-over bell rang and she watched John Peter follow his new friends.

"— I asked you, do you want another cookie?"

Nettie shook her head.

"It's time to line up —"

Nettie threw her empty milk carton into the rubbish and lined up with the other seventh-graders. Recognizing the back of John Peter's head, she called out to him.

"Are you deaf or something?" Josephine said, giving Nettie a gentle poke. "I asked you if you wanted to walk home with me."

Again Nettie shook her head. And again she called out to John Peter. But he was much too busy to hear her.

⇥ Chapter Sixteen ⇤

At the end of Nettie's and John Peter's first day of school, Mrs. Fiorey summoned them to the office to tell them the grandfather had called. "Something came up and he asks that you walk home with your neighbors, the Palmas. I asked them to wait at the front entrance for you."

John Peter usually got upset when plans changed like that, but all he did was talk about how nice his teacher was and how funny one of his new friends was. "I'm going to ask Pa if he can come over someday."

"You better not. Remember what Grandma Bessie said about old people. They like their peace and quiet."

"But Pa's different. He wouldn't mind. Besides, he's not that old."

"I'm telling you not to. But you do whatever you want." Nettie knew as soon as she said to do it, he wouldn't.

Josephine was waiting at the entrance, and when John

Peter saw the boy with her, he gave out a whoop. "That's my friend. That's Donnie. The funny one."

Nettie didn't think he was funny. All he did was burp and John Peter would practically fall on the ground laughing. And when he crossed his eyes, twirled his hair, and burped, John Peter laughed so hard, he hiccuped the way he used to when he was a baby.

Donnie stopped clowning when John Peter found out the lady in the window was his mother and asked him why she always sat there. Nettie couldn't hear what Donnie answered, but after a while, John Peter put his arm around him and said, "I wish my mother was sitting in a window."

That surprised Nettie. He was only a baby when she went away. It was always Nettie who told him about her, how much Nettie missed her —

"Natasha. Did you hear me? I said my mother is agoraphobic —"

"Oh, that's too bad."

"It's worse than bad. She never goes out. She's afraid of crowds and things."

"Like Mrs. Digby," Nettie said.

"Who's Mrs. Digby?"

Nettie wasn't about to tell a practical stranger they'd lived with Mrs. Digby and a thousand other people. "A neighbor in Ohio. She was afraid of everything until her husband made her go for help.

"Mama won't go for help." She called out to Donnie not to dare cross the street. "Me and my father, Donnie too, keep telling her she has to."

Nettie had the urge to correct her, but she stifled it.

When they turned the corner into Salem Street, Josephine waved over to her mother, then told Nettie she'd call for her on Monday. "Or maybe we can get together over the weekend." She took Donnie's hand and started across the street. "And don't call me Josephine. That's just for school. I'm Josie. Okay?"

"The first day is always the hardest," the grandfather said as he fixed them a snack. "But tomorrow is Saturday, the easiest day. *Giusto?*"

Nettie didn't think it was right. At Grandma Bessie's Saturday was the worst day of the week. There was the wash to do. The floors. The bathroom —

"It was your father's favorite day," he went on as he put cinnamon toast and hot cocoa in front of them. "Your grandmother would make his favorite breakfast. Zeppole. Do you know what zeppole are?" And without waiting for an answer, he said, "Fried dough. But what fried dough it was! Sprinkled with sugar, it was light enough to rise off the platter." He looked up. "I can still taste them, Anna."

He poured himself some coffee and sat at the table. "Then your grandmother would take your father to the library." He bit into a piece of toast. "I cannot make zeppole, but tomorrow we will go to the library to get cards for both of you."

But they never got there. The grandfather got a call early Saturday morning, and as soon as he put breakfast on the table, he announced he had some important business to attend to.

"I will be at this number if you need me," he said, handing Nettie a piece of paper. "Are you sure you will be all right for an hour? Two at most?"

All right? Nettie had been taking care of herself and John Peter for forever. She'd changed his diapers after Momma and Poppa went away. Gave him his bath. Nobody worried about her drowning him or dropping him on his head. And Nettie had been only six years old.

She wanted to tell him that, but all she said was "We'll be fine." And when he told her she was not to light the stove, she wanted to tell him it was her job to light the stove and cook every day at Grandma Bessie's, but all she did was nod and promise not to.

"Good," he said, satisfied. "Now lock the door behind me and do not open it for anybody. *Capisci?*"

"I understand," Nettie said. She'd quickly gotten used to his occasional lapses into Italian.

Nettie headed back to the kitchen and, remembering they were alone in the house, did something she often did when Grandma Bessie wasn't around. She danced. She danced and sang her way down the hallway and into the kitchen but stopped when she saw John Peter standing by the sink, licking a plate. "What are you doing with that?"

"Eating cheesecake."

Nettie yanked the plate out of his hand. "You don't

lick plates." She looked down at Cassie. "And you don't feed cats with the plates people use."

"She likes cheesecake and Pa says a cat's mouth is cleaner than ours."

"That's not true." She pulled the plate from underneath Cassie and ran it under hot water. "It's disgusting, and I don't want to see you licking plates either. If you did that at Grandma Bessie's, you know what would happen."

"I couldn't do anything there," John Peter said. "And besides, we never had anything delicious."

"Come on," Nettie said, clearing off her place at the table, "let's clear up the kitchen. Aunt Aleta is calling today. Maybe she'll decide to come over."

John Peter slumped into a chair. "I don't think I like her."

Nettie scooped up the silverware, tossed it into the dishpan, and turned on the hot water. "Why?"

"Because I think she's . . . I don't know the word . . . but it's when you're one thing and you want people to think you're something else —"

"Why do you say that?"

"Because of what she said on the telephone that day. Saying she was busy when she wasn't doing anything." Pretending to hold a telephone to his ear, he mimicked Aleta: " 'Let me check my schedule —' "

"Oh, that. She was just trying not to show how excited she was."

"Grandma Bessie used to do things like that. She'd say

she was too busy to talk to the teachers or go to School Night. Then she'd sit and smoke her cigar. Remember? You said that was lying —"

"It was."

"Well, how come what *she* did isn't lying —"

Nettie rinsed the silverware and put it in the drainer. She didn't know what to answer, so she handed him a dish towel and told him to stop talking and start working.

"Anyway, I don't like her." He got up and began to dry the dishes. "Pa's different. He doesn't do that."

Nettie handed him a plate. "Do what?"

"Fool people."

"How can you tell that?"

"Because Abraham Lincoln never lied and Pa looks like him."

"It was George Washington who never lied. And it isn't what people look like that makes you like them, it's how they behave."

John Peter shrugged. "Don't you like the way he sometimes says 'Sit down'?"

"What are you talking about now?"

"Pa says *'Sedetevi.'* I like it better than saying 'Sit down.'"

"It means the same thing," Nettie said, handing him the last plate. "It's just the Italian word for sit." She smiled at him. *"Capisci?"*

He nodded, flicking the dish towel across Nettie's bottom. "Sit down," he said, his voice deep in his throat.

"What did you do that for?"

"I'm telling you to sit down . . . before I knock you down," he said, laughing so hard he doubled over.

"What's the matter with you? Are you trying to act like your friend?"

When he finally stopped laughing, he said, "That's the way Grandma Bessie used to say it."

Nettie laughed along with him. "Do you miss her?"

He shook his head. "Do you?"

"No." She sighed and dumped the pan of water down the drain, then hung the pan on the hook underneath the sink.

Nettie finished wiping down the counters and dried her hands. Cassie was meowing at a bird perched on the fire escape. A tiny bit of sun streamed in the small window above the sink. A lightness washed over her. "Let's dance," she said, taking John Peter's hands in hers. Singing at the top of her voice, she swung him around the kitchen and down the hallway, finally collapsing on the sofa in the parlor.

They were quiet for a few minutes, catching their breath. "Pa needs a new sofa. This one sags."

"The springs are going," Nettie said. She looked around. "Everything is."

"Except us," John Peter said. "We're never going. Right, Nettie?"

Nettie thought a long minute before answering, remembering all that Aleta had said. "Right," she said, nodding slowly. "That's right, John Peter." Then she went to the hall and dialed the number she had committed to memory.

"Ms. Bianca's residence," a voice answered.

"Is she there?"

"Sorry. She won't be available until early evening. Would you care to leave a message?"

"Umm, just tell her Nettie, I mean, Natasha called and that, I . . . I just wanted to know what day I'll be seeing her next week."

Nettie put the phone down, so excited she could barely breathe. A maid! Aleta had a maid.

She stood for a long minute, relishing all that was to come. Sleepovers. Swan boats. Family. She sighed a most contented sigh, went back into the parlor, took John Peter's hands, pulled him to his feet, twirled him around, and in a voice sweet and pure sang, "Who said that every wish would be heard and answered when wished on the morning star?" She put her face close to his and said, "It sure wasn't Grandma Bessie."

⊰ CHAPTER SEVENTEEN ⊱

Just after the grandfather called to say he wouldn't be home until after four, the telephone rang again. John Peter ran to answer it, but Nettie beat him to it, sure it would be Aleta. It was Donnie.

"It's for you," Nettie said, handing John Peter the phone.

"For me?" he said, his eyes wide. "This is the first telephone call I ever got."

He cleared his throat. "Who is this?" He put his hand on the receiver, a smile covering his face, and whispered, "It's Donnie. My friend."

"Don't talk too long. Aunt Aleta is going to call."

John Peter nodded, then said, "You can come over?"

Nettie shook her head. "He can't come over. I'm not supposed to let anybody in. Besides, I don't want anybody —"

"But Pa said."

"How could he say?"

Again, he placed his hand over the receiver. "Pa's at Donnie's house. He's talking business with his father. Please, Nettie? Please?"

Nettie sighed her disgusted sigh. "Tell him no burping, or stuff like that. Understand?"

John Peter understood. Donnie didn't. Shoes off, hat and jacket flung to the floor, he picked up Cassie, motioned to John Peter, and the two of them disappeared down the hall.

Remembering she hadn't fed Cassie, Nettie filled her dish and did what the grandfather always did — tapped the dish on the floor and called out, "*Mangia,* Cassie" — and waited for the cat to come running.

When she didn't come, Nettie went looking for her. The doors leading to the bedrooms were closed. She looked in the grandfather's room, in John Peter's, finally in hers.

A light seeped out from under the closet door and when she opened it, Cassie flew out, one of Nettie's kneesocks wrapped around her tail.

"Get out of there," Nettie ordered. "This isn't a playground and Cassie isn't a stuffed toy."

Donnie shot out, sliding across the bedroom floor and into the hall, calling John Peter to join him. The two skated back and forth, John Peter laughing, Donnie burping. They ignored Nettie's pleas to calm down until Donnie reeled into the wall and one of the pictures came crashing down.

"Didn't I ask you to stop?" Nettie said. Ignoring Donnie's attempt to apologize, she picked up the picture of her father, its frame twisted, the glass broken. "You're going to have to leave. Now."

"No," John Peter said. "You're not the boss."

Nettie helped Donnie with his jacket and hat, handed him his shoes, and walked him to the door. "He's leaving."

"He is not."

"Don't worry," Donnie called as he ran down the stairs, shoeless. "I'll come back when your grandfather comes home."

"I'm calling Pa," John Peter shouted. "He'll let him stay." He started for the phone, but Nettie blocked the way.

"You are *not* calling anybody. And he's not staying."

"You're mean," John Peter shrieked. "Meaner than Grandma Bessie or anybody, and I hate you." He picked up one of his shoes and threw it at Nettie. "You hear me? I hate you."

"Get into your room."

"You spoil everything," John Peter said, sobbing. "I-I-I w-w-wish you weren't m-m-my s-s-sister." He turned and ran down the hall, slamming the door so hard, Nettie felt the floor vibrate.

She stood, motionless. Numb. John Peter had stuttered. What he'd said didn't matter. Throwing his shoe at her didn't matter. He'd stuttered talking to her.

She picked up his shoes and slowly walked down the hall to his room. "John Peter," she said, "open the door. Please."

"No."

"I'm sorry."

"No, you're not. You sent my friend away and he said he was sorry and you're not. You're glad."

"I'm not glad."

"You don't want me to have any friends. You don't even want me to like Pa just 'cause you don't like him, and you don't want to stay."

"That's not true. I do like him. And I want to stay. Really I do. Open the door. Please?"

A long minute passed. The door opened. "You do?"

Nettie nodded.

"You're sure?"

Again, she nodded.

He smiled.

"I'm sorry I yelled at you." She gave him a hard hug.

"That's okay," he said, hugging her back. "You want to see something?"

"Did you go poking?"

"No. Donnie and me found it."

"Donnie and I," she said, following him into her room.

"Look, Nettie," he said, pointing to the back of the closet door. "It says 'John Peter, February 1, 1961, two years old.'" He took Nettie's arm and gently tugged her closer. "And here, it says 'John Peter, February 1, 1967, eight years old.' That's Poppa's birthday. Right?"

She nodded. She'd opened and closed the closet door every day since they'd come, and she hadn't seen this. She ran her hand up and down the markings. "Poppa at twelve. Poppa at thirteen. At fourteen." She inched her fingers up to the last marking. "Poppa at seventeen," she whispered.

"Why did they do this?"

Nettie knew. She once saw a movie where the parents measured their children every year to see how they'd grown. The mother would stand them with their backs against the kitchen wall while the father made the mark. "Because they loved Poppa," she said, pressing herself against the door, closing her eyes, imagining her father standing where she stood now, his mother gently holding his head, his father carefully making the mark. A warm, sweet feeling swept over her.

"My turn," John Peter said, pushing Nettie aside, positioning himself against the door. "Look! I'm taller than Poppa was when he was nine."

"And look, Nettie," his voice squealed with pleasure, "I'm taller than Poppa when he was ten and I'm only eight." He looked closer. "Yep. I'm taller than Poppa. How is that, Nettie? How can I be taller than Poppa was?"

"I think Poppa took after his mother. From her pictures, she doesn't look too tall. Grandma Bessie is tall, so is Pa —" The word had slipped out so easily.

"You called him Pa, Nettie. You did. You called him Pa."

Nettie smiled. "I did, didn't I?"

"And we're staying." John Peter held out his pinkie. "Promise?"

She linked her pinkie in his. "Promise."

They took turns measuring themselves, John Peter

laughing, Nettie serious, her mind flitting from the grandfather to Aleta. They couldn't go back the way they always did because, despite Nettie's promise to herself, she liked — more than liked — the grandfather. She knew that if he could, he would let them stay. But the other day she had heard him on the phone saying how worried he was about money. How things were piling up. How he had to get a job somehow. It scared Nettie.

Aleta had to help. She just had to.

⇥ Chapter Eighteen ⇤

Nettie woke to the sound of rain beating on the window and that of her stomach growling. Not from hunger. From fear.

Every morning for the last few weeks, the grandfather had been leaving the apartment when Nettie and John Peter left for school. He was home before school was out, but he'd given Nettie a key. "In the event I'm delayed," he'd said. He hadn't actually told them what he was doing, but Nettie knew. He was looking for a job. Even though it heightened her fear, Nettie listened when he talked on the phone. Just the other night she'd heard him say he didn't know where to go next. "Nobody wants a sixty-year-old former undertaker." He'd laughed when he said it.

But last night he didn't laugh. "I do not know what will happen if I do not get something soon. The children need so many things. It is not easy."

That's how it always used to be. Needing things. Not having the money. Then back to Grandma Bessie.

But this time, Nettie was determined that, no matter what, they were not leaving. Putting her feet on the cold floor, she yawned and stretched, and then she remembered her dream.

In the dream, Aleta had called and asked Nettie to meet her in the park, telling her she had something important to tell her. Nettie had put her coat on over her nightgown, slipped into her shoes, and started down the hall, but the grandfather blocked her way. Nettie begged and pleaded for him to let her go, and when he finally did, Nettie couldn't move from where she stood. She tried lifting up one foot and then the other, but neither would move.

"Time to get up," the grandfather called. "It is getting late."

Nettie got out of bed and walked down to the bathroom, still thinking about the dream. Grandma Bessie always said dreams were visions of things to come. Maybe that's what the dream was, a sign that Aleta would call. Lately she hadn't called, and whenever Nettie called her, the maid would say how busy Aleta was and that she would give her the message.

The dream was a sign. She will call, and she won't tell me how busy she is. Or how sorry she is, or that she'll be seeing me and then not come. She will come.

Nettie didn't care about having high tea, or browsing in the shops, or seeing Louisburg Square. She just wanted to ask Aleta, straight out, to help them stay.

"Natasha. John Peter," the grandfather called again. "I have an appointment at nine. Hurry."

"Coming," Nettie said, running the comb through her hair one last time.

In the kitchen, the grandfather's music played. Since Nettie had joined the chorus at school, he played opera music. "Anna and I always had music in the house, but she took the music with her," he told them. "But you have brought it back."

John Peter scooped out a small amount of cat food from the sack under the counter. "What's an agnostiphobic, Pa?" he asked, setting Cassie's bowl on the floor.

"I never heard that term. Perhaps you mean agnostic. That is somebody who denies the existence of God."

The grandfather placed a bowl of fruit on the table. "Natasha, would you get the cereal from the pantry? Time is growing short."

"Why would that make her sit in the window?"

"What are you talking about?" Nettie asked, handing the cereal to the grandfather.

"Donnie's mother. He said she's agnostiphobic and that's why she sits in the window."

Nettie sighed her exasperated sigh. "There's no such thing as an agnostiphobic. It's *agoraphobic*. His mother is agoraphobic."

"But why does it make her sit in the window?"

"Because she's afraid to go out. Of being in crowded places —"

"She doesn't mind crowds. Donnie told me he can have his whole class to his party."

Nettie took a mouthful of cereal.

"Less talk, John Peter, more eating." The grandfather

glanced out the window. "It is coming down hard." He shook his head. "Ahh, if I hadn't lost my car, rain would be no problem for us."

"Where did you lose it?" John Peter asked.

"It is a long story. Now finish your breakfast."

The telephone rang. Nettie leapt up from the table but the grandfather motioned for her to sit. "I will answer. You finish your breakfast."

Nettie sat on the edge of her chair, waiting to hear the magical words, "Natasha, come. It is your aunt Aleta." Instead the grandfather came back into the kitchen and said, "From my mouth to God's ear and from God's mouth to Mr. Palma's ear. He is driving you to school." The grandfather got their lunches out of the refrigerator, gave them their milk money, and hurried them out the door. "If I should not be here this afternoon, have your snack, then do your homework. *Capite?*

"Say hello to your friends," he called after them. "And remember to thank Mr. Palma."

Nettie did just that. Then, settling into the backseat of Mr. Palma's car, she smiled at the thought of Josie being her friend. Her best friend. For a while after Nettie sent Donnie home, Josie barely spoke to her. And when she finally did, she was still angry. "Why did you do that to Donnie?"

"He was running around, Josephine, and he wouldn't listen to me."

"What are you, his grandmother? He's only a little kid who acts up a lot because he doesn't understand about

112

my mother. You should be glad he likes John Peter so much. And cut out calling me Josephine."

"Why?"

I've told you before, I'm only Josephine in school. That's why."

"I didn't mean that. I mean, why should I be glad Donnie likes John Peter?"

Josie shook her head. "Because kids need friends. Everybody does. Even an old fart like you."

Nettie had turned on her heel, telling Josie how disgusting she was and that she didn't care to be in her company. But as the days wore on, and John Peter insisted on walking to and from school with Donnie, Josie wore down Nettie's armor until Nettie allowed her in.

"Yoo-hoo," Josie said, poking Nettie. "Natasha DeAngelus. Come to the world of the living. We're at school."

Nettie thanked Mr. Palma, again, and together she and Josie started toward their first class. Music. Nettie's favorite. Just yesterday, Mr. Caputo had asked her to try out for the lead soprano in the annual Young People's Concert.

Nettie refused, but when she told the grandfather, he urged her to audition. "You have the voice of an angel. You can do it."

But, this morning, it was Josie who persuaded her.

"I'm trying out for alto," Josie said as they walked into the music room. She looked around, then whispered, "I made a pact with my mother. If I get it, she'll come.

"You try, Natasha. Please. John Peter told me you've been wanting to see the Gardner Museum."

"What's that got to do with trying out?"

"It's there. The concert. That's where they have it."

"You mean I'd get to sing there?"

"If the Music Committee chooses you. Helen Brown and Irene DeBenedictis are trying out, but I'll bet anything you'll get it. Mr. Caputo says you've got perfect pitch."

"My grandfather says that only means you're able to recognize A when you hear it, but it doesn't prove that you're musical."

When the music class was over and Mr. Caputo dismissed them, he asked Nettie to step up to his desk. Josie followed.

"Did you make up your mind to try out for the concert?" he asked.

Josie poked her. "Say yes."

"Yes."

"Wonderful," Mr. Caputo said. "This afternoon we meet here and begin to work."

And they did work. They went over the same piece of music so many times that Donnie and John Peter were long gone when practice was finally over.

All the way home, Josie talked about how much she needed to get the part. "What if I don't get it?"

"You will. You heard him say how great you sounded."

"That was Mr. Caputo, but I heard Miss Cottrell is

going to be on the committee, and you know who she'll pick."

Without waiting for an answer, Josie said, "She'll hold out for one of her pets. You just wait."

"It's not the part I want as much as I want Mama to come. Papa says if she doesn't leave the house soon, we'll have to bomb the house to get her out.

"I told him that wasn't funny," Josie went on. "That she needed help, but he says in her own time, she'll go for help. That we just have to be patient and love her the way she is. I do love her the way she is, but I told him it wasn't right just letting her sit there. Do you know how many fights Donnie's gotten into because of my mother?"

Again, the way Josie did when she had something important to say, she didn't wait for Nettie to answer.

"Too many to count. The kids call her the picture in the window. 'Is your mother the Mona Lisa of Salem Street?' the kids ask him. So he fights."

"That's who it is," Nettie said.

"What are you talking about?"

"The Mona Lisa. At my grandmother's there was a calendar with her picture on it. I remember reading about her, too." Nettie looked up, closed her eyes, and concentrated. "Underneath the picture it said, 'Her smile is not a total smile, but a smile that expresses the doubts hidden in the human spirit.'" She turned to Josie. "Donnie shouldn't be ashamed of that —"

"Are you for real? You think he cares about the human spirit? I guess if she was somebody else's mother he might. But not when it's your own mother."

"I wouldn't mind."

"That's what you say because she's not your mother."

"That's not so, Josie. I really wouldn't care."

But Josie was too busy waving to her mother at the window to answer Nettie. "John Peter is here with Donnie," her mother called. "Come have some raisin bread."

Nettie shook her head. "I can't. I told my grandfather I'd make the salad. He may be late. Thank you anyway."

And from the window: "Tomorrow, then."

"Tomorrow."

Nettie hadn't told the grandfather she'd make a salad, but today she didn't want to go to Josie's. Josie was her best friend, but even she didn't understand. Nettie *wouldn't* care if her mother never made bread or zeppole. Wouldn't mind if all she did was sit in the window, or if the kids called her the Mona Lisa. As long as she was there. Waiting.

⫷ CHAPTER NINETEEN ⫸

There was a note on the kitchen table from the grand-father, telling Nettie he would be home at five. "Natasha, you and John Peter get your homework finished. I will bring something home for supper. Please feed Cassie . . ."

Nettie was about to fill Cassie's bowl when the phone rang.

"Hello," she said. Hearing the voice on the other end, her face flushed with excitement. "Aleta! Hello."

"Hello yourself. What are you up to?"

"I just got back from school."

"Where's Frank?"

"Out on business."

"What business? Monkey business?" She laughed.

"He's looking for a job."

"Still? He's been doing that for a while. But I guess nobody wants to hire a man his age."

"He's not that old —"

"Well, he's not young. But enough about him. How'd you like to come on over here?"

Like it? Nettie's heart pounded. The dream *had* been a sign.

"I'd love that, but I don't know whether I can."

"Why?"

"My grandfather might not like it."

"Oh, poo. Just leave him a note telling him where you are. He won't mind. Besides, I need a little company. I'm down. Down. Down."

"Why?"

"Well, I've been on three auditions this week and I've got another one tomorrow —"

"That's good, isn't it?"

"Well, sure. But it's not with Hannah Macklin." She signed. "So, Natasha, are you coming or not?"

"Are you sure he won't mind?"

"Listen, hon, Frank's so forgetful, he'll forget what he told you. Just kidding. But really, sweetheart, he won't mind. Trust me."

"I don't know —"

"Do I lie? Come on. I'll have Sarkus — remember him? My agent, the man in the pink truck — pick you up. Don't let him do any deliveries. I need to pick out an outfit for the audition. You hear? Don't forget. I'm going to track him down with my beeper right now, so you get on outside and wait for him —"

"I've got to get John Peter. He's at his friend's."

"Oh . . . maybe he can stay at his friend's and you and I can spend time alone —"

"I don't think so. I'll call him right now."

"Suit yourself. And, oh, one last thing. You know the dresser by the closet in Frank's room . . . well, do you?"

"Yes."

"Good. Do me a favor. Look in the bottom drawer, toward the back . . . there should be a long black velvet box. Will you bring it to me?"

"I don't think I should look —"

"Look, they're my sister's pearls. I only want to borrow them for the audition. Frank won't mind. Anna wanted me to have them anyway. Now hurry up. I'm calling Sarkus now."

Click. Dial tone. Gone.

An uneasiness came over Nettie. The way Aleta didn't really want John Peter . . . and saying the grandfather was old and forgetful . . . and the pearls. But Nettie dismissed her feelings, trying to convince herself that the dream *had* been a sign. She dialed Donnie's number and told John Peter to get right home.

Then she went into the grandfather's room, again trying to believe that her dream *was* a vision. That Aleta would come to their rescue. Opening the bottom drawer, she assured herself that she wasn't really poking but doing a favor for Aleta. That the grandfather wouldn't mind. Slipping her hand underneath some linen, she found the box.

"What are you doing?" John Peter stood in the doorway, peeling a banana. "You told me not to poke."

"I'm not poking. I was getting something for Aunt Aleta. She wants us to come to visit her."

"I don't want to visit her," John Peter said, biting off a piece of banana and twirling the peel.

"We have to. She's sending Sarkus to pick us up."

"But what about Pa?"

"Aleta told me to leave him a note, telling him where we are."

"I'm not going."

"Oh yes you are. Sarkus is picking us up in two minutes."

"I am not," he said, still twirling the peel. "I'm waiting for Pa."

Still feeling uncomfortable about what Aleta had said, but using everything she could to get him to go, Nettie said, "She said Pa is getting forgetful and he won't remember what he told us."

"She's got no right to say that about Pa," John Peter said. "I told you she wasn't nice." He stuffed the banana peel into his back pocket. "And I can tell you lots more stuff about her."

"What stuff?"

"Like she's the one who made Pa lose his business, because she made up old people like they were going to dance on the stage or something. She said even old people should go out in style."

"What old people?"

"The dead old people."

"How would you know that?" Even as she asked, Nettie knew he'd been poking.

"Then a lady sued Pa because Aleta dyed her

husband's hair black and when the lady came back to the funeral parlor, she didn't even know her own husband."

"Stop it," Nettie said, taking John Peter's arm. "Listen to me. You did exactly what Grandma Bessie told you not to do."

"I did not." He tried to wiggle from her grasp, but Nettie held on.

"I said to listen."

"Let go. I didn't go poking. You're the one who's poking." John Peter pulled his arm free and headed toward the kitchen. "My friend told me."

Nettie made a grab for his pants but all she got hold of was the banana peel. John Peter scooted down the hall, Nettie slipping and sliding behind him, but before she caught up, he rushed into his room and slammed the door.

"You mean Donnie?" Nettie yelled. "What does he know about anything?"

"He knows a lot about everything. He knows how Pa lost his car and his business and everything. All because of her."

"He's a liar."

"She's the liar."

Nettie gave the door a hard rap. "Open this door. Now."

"No."

"John Peter, we've got to go. Pa has no job. We'll have to go back to Grandma Bessie if Aleta doesn't help —"

"I'd rather go back to Grandma Bessie than live with her —"

"I don't mean live with her. I mean she could help us. Help Pa. Come on. Answer me . . . Okay, I'm going, and you'll be all alone."

"I don't care."

John Peter, who never wanted to be alone, meant what he said. Nettie knew that. And she knew leaving him was something she shouldn't do, but she had to go.

Nettie rapped one last rap on John Peter's door, pleaded one last plea, threatened one last threat, then turned and hurried down the stairs, out the door, and into the waiting truck.

⊰ Chapter Twenty ⊱

From the minute Nettie left John Peter locked in his room until the grandfather stormed through the "drawing room" at Aleta's she realized coming to see Aleta had been a mistake. A big one.

Sarkus dropped her off in front of Aleta's, telling her to wait inside while he parked. Standing at the curb, Nettie was puzzled. *This isn't Louisburg Square. This isn't anywhere near the Square.* And she was more than puzzled by the sign over the door: "Actors' Residence — All Who Enter These Doors Are Welcome." Even before she got inside, Nettie heard voices. Lots of them. A piano being played. Somebody singing.

"I'm over here, Natasha." Aleta waved and put her hand over the telephone receiver. "I'll be just another minute." Taking her hand off, she said, "Aleta Bianca here. Any messages? Are you sure? Would you check again? I'm expecting one from the coast."

Again Aleta put her hand over the receiver. "Go on

in," she said, motioning with her chin. "Sit down. You, too, Sarkus. Be right with you."

But she wasn't. She made one phone call after another. People wandered in and out of the "drawing room," as Sarkus told Nettie it was called by everybody who lived there. "It's a fancy word for living room." He leaned over and whispered, "It was Allie's idea."

"Why does she live here?"

Sarkus rubbed his thumb over his fingers. "She's a little short of money right now. Like everybody here, she's waiting for her big chance." He pointed his finger at Allie. "One day she'll be a big star and have her footprints outside Grauman's Chinese."

Nettie sighed a very long sigh. Aleta had no maid. It had only been an answering service, like the one the Digbys had. When was she going to learn? When was that part of her going to take over, that part of her that knew things were not going to be fine, were not going to be the way she wanted them?

"Did you bring the dress, Sarkus?" Aleta said, putting down the phone and starting up the stairs, calling for Nettie to follow.

"I've got no black dresses on the truck."

"What do you mean? I told you two weeks ago that I needed one. Remember? For the audition? The cosmetic spot? The one you arranged."

"Tomorrow maybe I pick one up," Sarkus said, his hand on the doorknob. "Now I have to do my deliveries."

"Tomorrow's too late," Aleta called after him. "What

do I have you as an agent for? You're supposed to take care of these things."

"I'll take care. Don't worry." The door closed behind him.

"You'd better!"

Nettie was halfway up the stairs when the door burst open and she heard the grandfather's voice. "Aleta," he bellowed. "I need to speak to you."

Passing Nettie on the stairs, he said, "Wait for me downstairs." It was more an order than anything else, and he didn't look at her but kept his eyes focused on Aleta.

"What is it, Frank?"

"You have to ask?"

Nettie watched as the grandfather followed Aleta upstairs. Her door slammed.

A woman ran up the stairs and knocked on Aleta's door. "You know the rules. When there's a man in the room, the door stays open, at least six inches from the doorjamb. This is a respectable place."

"He's my brother-in-law."

"I don't care who he is, the door stays open."

Hoping to hear what was going on, Nettie took one step up, then another. Still another until she was halfway up. Checking to see if anybody was watching, she tucked herself against the wall and listened.

"How can you say that?" Aleta said. "These are my sister's children. Don't I have any rights?"

The grandfather's voice. "You have rights, but not the

right to have them disobey me. And not the right to have my grandchild drive around in that truck.

"You know my feelings about that. Believe me, Aleta, you ask for trouble the way you use that man's business for your own purposes. You know he would do anything you ask, and you take advantage of that. You put him at risk —"

"He's my agent. And besides, there's nothing wrong —"

"Nothing wrong? You see nothing wrong with taking people's clothes?"

"Borrow. Not take. Borrow."

"I promised Anna to look after you, but you make that difficult. Impossible. I wash my hands of it. Remember that if you get dragged into court. I have enough worries doing what I will have to do with these children. I will not have them exposed —"

What does he mean by that? What will he have to do with us?

"Don't waste your time worrying about me. I'm about to hit the big one and when I do, I'll be able to buy and sell the swanky shops that Sarkus's ritzy bitch customers —"

"I am leaving —"

Nettie scooted down the stairs.

"Dear old pure-of-heart Frank can't take language like that coming from ladies." The door slammed, then opened. "Frank. Wait. Before you leave, do you want to know what your real problem is? You're still pissed off at me — excuse me, ladies don't get pissed — you're still angry because you think I was responsible for your business failing. I'll take part of the blame but not all of it, because the truth is, the day Anna took sick you turned into a zombie, and you were like that until the day Bessie wrote to say those kids were coming —"

The grandfather started down the stairs.

"Isn't that true, Frank?" she called out. "Give me that much —"

He stopped.

"I never said it was all your doing, but the lawsuit coming down on me was no help."

"There you go. Bringing up that damn lawsuit. What did she have to complain about? Her husband looking better than he ever did?"

"And there *you* go, still not seeing what you did was wrong."

"I still can't see what was so wrong with making that old guy look better going out of this world than he looked when he was here."

"You never see what you do as wrong. It is always the other person's doing. Just as you did when Sarkus's customer saw you wearing her dress —"

"He made it up to her. He gave her free cleaning —"

"For the rest of her life. And still you see nothing wrong with his assuming the responsibility. And the cost."

"He's my agent. That's what he gets paid for."

The grandfather threw up his hands. "Have it your

way. You always do. But it will be my way when it comes to these children."

"Okay. I made a mistake. But don't let this keep me from seeing them. Anna would want me to."

The grandfather continued down the stairs, took Nettie's arm, and headed out the door.

"Frank," Aleta called. "I'll call you. You, too, Natasha. I'll call you. You hear me? I'll call."

ᗒ CHAPTER TWENTY-ONE ᗕ

As Nettie sat in the back of a strange car, the grand-father at the wheel, waves of emotion swept over her. Humiliation. Fear. Confusion.

What exactly did Pa say? That we were a worry and he has to do something with us? What? The only thing he can. Send us back. Living with a hundred people in a dilapidated home for actors, Aleta can't help.

She wondered where John Peter was but was afraid to ask. She wondered where the grandfather had borrowed the car. She wondered when they'd be leaving.

Not a word was spoken from the time they left Aleta's until they pulled into the alleyway behind the grand-father's and into a garage underneath the building.

"Come," he said, once out of the car, "we need to talk before John Peter comes back." He led her from the garage through what was once the funeral parlor.

A hollow feeling gripped Nettie's stomach.

"You should not have left him," he said, his voice stern. "You know that?"

Nettie nodded. "Where is he?"

"With the Palmas." He opened the door to the stairs leading to the apartment.

In the kitchen, the grandfather put out bread and cheese and some apples, poured Nettie a glass of milk, and the two of them sat down. "Eat. You must be hungry."

But she wasn't.

"Well, then it is time we talked."

Nettie wanted to put her hands over her ears, not listen to what she knew was coming.

The grandfather took in a deep breath, let it out slowly. "Natasha, you and John Peter have been here only a short time. Perhaps because he is younger and adapts more easily —"

That wasn't true. John Peter usually found it harder to settle in than she ever did.

"— accepts people and change. But you —"

Nettie leapt up from the table. "I won't go without him. I won't. He comes with me."

"What are you talking about?"

"I won't go back to Grandma Bessie's without him. Momma said I have to take care of him. We stay together."

"Of course you will stay together. Who said you were not going to?"

Something strange happened to Nettie. Something she never allowed herself to do when anybody else could see. Or hear. She began to cry.

"What is it?" the grandfather asked. "What have I said to upset you like this?"

She couldn't speak. She bit her lip, trying to get control of herself.

The grandfather looked away, as though he understood her shame. He turned his head slightly, lifted his chin a bit, narrowed his eyes, and waited until Nettie calmed herself.

"Natasha, it is not my intent to upset you," he said, still not looking at her, "but I must tell you how I feel.

"When you first came, I felt a strong barrier. One that I could not seem to break through. It was different with John Peter. He saw me for what I was. A lonely old man who had been given another chance. That barrier has broken down somewhat, but still I feel a resistance in you." He reached out to take Nettie's hand, but she pulled away. "Why do you do that?"

"Because . . . because —"

"Go on."

"Because I'm afraid —"

"Of what?"

Nettie took a deep breath. "Of going back."

"Why would you be afraid of that? Have I given you reason to think that?"

"We always go back. Grandma Bessie always says the money is in the mail —"

"What money?"

"The money she always promises to send. The money she promised Cousin Jen and Renchie. All of you —"

"She has promised me no money."

Nettie's chin fell to her chest, the way John Peter's did. She wanted to punch herself, the way she wanted to punch him when he cried in front of Grandma Bessie.

"That's because she thinks you're rich."

"Rich? Why would she think that?"

"Because she said you owned a flower emporium and anybody who owned one had to be rich."

"A flower emporium? Where did she —"

"It's not fair. Always being sent back." She wiped her nose on her sleeve. "We're not boomerangs. We're people. You hear?"

He nodded. Handed her a napkin. Said very softly, "I hear. But now hear me. It is different this time."

"No, it's not. It's always the same. I heard you tell Aleta that all you have are worries wondering what to do with us —"

"Yes. That is right. To bring up children is a worry —"

Cassie made a leap from the windowsill into the grandfather's lap. He rubbed her back, pulled her ear gently. "But worry or not, you and John Peter will not go back —"

"But you don't have money —"

"Ahh! So I send you back? Is that how it works?" He shook his finger back and forth. "No. No. No. I am the grandfather," he said pounding his chest with his fingers. "You are the child. It is not for you to worry where the money will come from." He reached out and took her hand. Nettie didn't pull back.

He looked up. "I am making progress, Anna."

He squeezed her hand. "You and John Peter are my child's children. Part of me. You will not go back."

He placed Cassie in Nettie's arms, took the napkin from her hand, and wiped her cheeks. "Now, come, Natasha, it is time we go for your brother."

That night, like the first night she'd come, Nettie lay in bed unable to sleep. She curled up, her head burrowed into the pillows, a little afraid to let all of her believe they were really staying. That this was her room. This was her bed. These pillows, hers.

She thought about Aleta. Thought about what the grandfather had said when Nettie told him about the pearls. "Aleta does not think before she acts, never thinks of what her actions do to others." He'd slapped his forehead. "She needs someone to take charge. Perhaps Sarkus is the one to do what Anna and I could not."

Nettie thought about how the grandfather said he was the one in charge of them now. She felt good about that, but that part deep inside her — the part that clung to the idea that one day Momma and Poppa would come back and they'd be in charge again — crept back.

The streetlight cast a ribbon of light into the room and across the door to her closet. Images of her father and mother flickered before her — her father laying his hand on Nettie's feverish forehead . . . her mother placing a cool cloth on Nettie's hot cheeks . . . her mother holding out her arms to catch John Peter when he took his first step . . . her father cheering when he did.

Nettie tried to hold on to them, but like stars when the night sky first meets the pale light of morning, they disappeared.

⊰ Chapter Twenty-two ⊱

Things were happening so fast, Nettie's head spun. Two days earlier, the grandfather had gotten a job. Josie's uncle, a funeral director in downtown Boston, hired him to drive one of his limousines. Relief washed over Nettie; they *would* stay.

She even let go a bit of her other big concern, that of the funeral business becoming a reality. Josie had told her that going back into the funeral business was expensive. "My uncle says one casket can cost three thousand dollars, and when you're in business you need tons of them."

Then the day before, Aleta called to apologize to the grandfather. The grandfather closed his eyes, nodded his head, and sighed the longest sigh Nettie ever heard. "Yes, Aleta, yes, I accept your apology." He shrugged and handed the telephone to Nettie.

Aleta told Nettie how sorry she was for asking her to take Anna's pearls without the grandfather's permission.

"I'll be returning them tomorrow. Maybe we can spend some time together."

John Peter still thought she was a phony, but Nettie tried not to think that way. And when Aleta said for the hundredth time "I'll call before I come, Natasha," Nettie believed she would.

And today was the long-awaited day Nettie was to try out for the soprano lead in the Young People's Concert. Before they had left practice the day before, Mr. Caputo had instructed them to make sure to get enough rest, but Nettie had been too excited to sleep. They had celebrated the grandfather's job with Josie's family, eating Josie's mother's zeppole, drinking cappuccino.

"These are wonderful, Daria," the grandfather had teased. "But —"

Josie's mother laughed. "I know Frank. Anna's were so light they floated off the platter."

But the celebration wasn't the only reason Nettie got no sleep. Every time she closed her eyes, she saw herself at the tryouts. Saw herself trip on the stairs leading to the stage. Worried that she'd open her mouth to sing and nothing would come out.

Nettie was just about to get out of bed when the grandfather poked his head into her room. "I must leave. Mr. Palma called early this morning, one of his drivers is sick and I am to take his place." He adjusted his tie and put his jacket on. "I left breakfast on the table. See that you and John Peter eat." He smiled a broad smile. "*Buona fortuna*, Natasha. You will sing like a nightingale today."

136

Nettie quickly dressed and got John Peter to eat breakfast. She tried to force down a banana but couldn't. She fed Cassie, got their lunches from the refrigerator, took milk money from the coffee can, and locked the door after them.

The day was bright and a light breeze blew in from the harbor. Josie was waiting for her. "What kept you?" she called, crossing over with Donnie to meet Nettie and John Peter.

"My grandfather left for work early, and I had a lot to do."

"I'm nervous," Josie said. "I feel so sick to my stomach, I don't think I'll make it until two o'clock."

And she didn't. She vomited during second period and again during fourth. And when she said she had a pain in her stomach, the school nurse called her father to come pick her up.

Nettie got permission from the nurse to sit with Josie until her father came.

"You know I don't care about the concert," Josie said, tears running down her cheeks. "I really don't. It's my mother. She's got nothing to come out for now."

Nettie tried to comfort her. Tried to tell her everything would be fine. That her mother would come out. "She will. I just know that."

But Josie just shook her head. "Not unless a miracle happens."

The rest of the day dragged by and when the time finally came, and Nettie sat waiting her turn, her thoughts turned to Josie. *Maybe if I get the lead, Josie and I can talk her mother into coming to see me.* Then she wondered what it would be like to be the one chosen, to be standing backstage at the museum, waiting to be called. To peek out from behind the velvet curtain to see who was in the audience. To smooth her hair. To check the buttons on her dress —

What dress? I don't have a dress, only skirts and blouses and two old pilly sweaters. Maybe I can borrow one from Josie. Or maybe Aleta. But Pa probably wouldn't let me do that. He'd think it was from Sarkus's truck —

"Natasha, you're next," Mr. Caputo said. "Don't be nervous. You'll do just fine." All sounds seemed to stop except the sound of Nettie's heart pounding in her ears. She made her way to the stage, carefully climbed the stairs, stood beside the piano, took a deep breath, and let it out slowly, just the way the grandfather had told her to do. She prayed that when Mr. Caputo gave her the signal to begin singing, her voice would cooperate.

It did, and when she sang the last note, Mr. Caputo smiled and nodded his head, the way he did when he was satisfied with a student's work. He told Nettie he'd know by the end of the day who had been chosen, then called Helen Brown's name and said, "Don't be nervous, Helen. You'll do just fine."

Nettie went back to her regular classes until the final bell rang, then gathered her books and started home.

As she turned into Salem Street, Mrs. Palma called out to her. "Where are Donnie and John Peter?"

"At band practice. They should be home by four. How is Josie?"

"Her father took her to the doctor."

"I'll come over to see her when she gets home."

"Call first. I don't want you to come if she's contagious. Your grandfather has enough to do without you being sick."

The door to the apartment was open. Nettie was sure she'd locked it that morning. She put her book bag on a chair, checked to see that Cassie hadn't gotten out, and was about to clear off the table when she saw a piece of paper propped against a glass half filled with juice.

Nettie picked it up, and even though it had the grandfather's name written across the front, she unfolded it and began to read.

Dear Frank —

Sorry you weren't here when I came by to pick up my old makeup case. Sarkus and I are on our way to New York. Just got word from Hannah Macklin. She wants me to try out for the part. And I don't trust anybody to do my makeup but me!

Hope you don't mind if I take Anna's pearls for luck. I'll return them as soon as the audition is over. Promise.

Wish me luck and tell Natasha I'll call her from New York. Promise that, too.

Aleta

Cassie wrapped herself around Nettie's legs, meowing to be fed. "How could she have left the door open for you to run off?" Nettie gently pulled Cassie's ear the way the grandfather always did. "Pa would die without you." She filled Cassie's bowl, tapped it gently on the floor, and said, "*Mangia*, Cassie. *Mangia*."

Seating herself at the kitchen table, Nettie read Aleta's note again. *Pa tried to tell me. John Peter, too. She says things she doesn't mean. Like taking us all those places. Bringing back the pearls.*

Nettie thought about what the grandfather had told her when she'd gone to Aleta's without his permission. "Aleta is like a spoiled, selfish child," he'd said. "And the sooner you accept her the way she is, the less you will be disappointed." He'd cupped Nettie's chin in his hand. "And the better your stomach will feel. Less *acido*.

"People are not made to our specifications, Natasha. When our expectations are not met, it leads to disappointment."

"Not always," Nettie said, folding the note and propping it against the napkin holder. She took the half-filled glass of orange juice to the sink and poured it down the drain. Then, looking around the kitchen she had come to love, she whispered, "Not always."

⊰ CHAPTER TWENTY-THREE ⊱

Nettie busied herself setting the table, taking the sauce from the refrigerator, and filling the pasta pot with water and placing it on the back burner, same as she'd been doing ever since the grandfather began to look for work. But since he'd looked so tired the night before when he got home, Nettie decided to surprise him. Even though it was early, she'd start supper. Have it waiting for him. Serve him. Later, she'd make cappuccino. So for the third time since they'd arrived, Nettie disobeyed him. She turned on the gas and lit the stove.

Nettie was about to adjust the burners when the phone rang. She called out to John Peter but remembered he was at band practice. She tossed the oven mitt to the side of the stove and hurried down the hall.

"Natasha," Mr. Caputo said, his voice ringing with excitement, "we just posted the list of solo parts. You made it. You've got the lead soprano part.

"Did you hear me, Natasha?"

Nettie heard but couldn't speak; she could scarcely breathe. *Wait till Pa hears. Wait till he hears.*

"Natasha? Are you there?"

"Yes. Yes. Thank you. Thank you."

"Remember, rehearsal after school tomorrow and every day for the next month. Congratulations."

She mumbled a thank-you and placed the phone back on the receiver. The feelings that rushed through her were some she hadn't felt in a long, long time. "I did it," she shouted as she twirled around and around and around until she was so dizzy she fell onto the sofa. She wanted to run to the front window and call out to everybody passing by. But first, she had to tell Pa. From downstairs, Nettie thought she heard the sound of the garage door opening, the whir of the limousine's motor.

"Pa! Pa! I did it," she shrieked as she flung the sitting room door open and flew down the stairs. "I'm the lead. You said I could do it and I did."

But when she got to the ground floor and opened the door to the garage, it was empty. Deflated, Nettie turned and started up the stairs. Before she got halfway up, she knew something was terribly wrong. Smoke seeped out from under the kitchen door and by the time she reached the landing, smoke poured from the parlor door and into the hall. She turned and ran back down the stairs and opened the outside door, hoping the air would clear the hall, shouting for help, screaming to Cassie as she raced back up the stairs.

The smoke thickened. Nettie's nose burned. Her eyes teared. Her throat tightened. Lifting her blouse and putting it over her nose and mouth, she reached the landing and opened the door to the kitchen. "Cassie. Cassie," she cried.

In the distance Nettie heard the whine of sirens and then minutes later firemen were all around, hoses spraying water everywhere, the sound of glass breaking, more water pouring through the windows. One of the firemen picked up Nettie and started down the stairs. She kicked and screamed and called for Cassie, but he wouldn't listen. She beat her fists against his chest, crying over and over, "Pa's cat. I've got to get Pa's cat."

She managed to squirm from his grip and started back up the stairs, but he stopped her, picked her up, and once outside held her fast. Over and over she cried out for Cassie.

"Where is your grandfather?" somebody asked, wrapping a coat around Nettie.

Nettie didn't answer. "I'll take care of her," the somebody said. "I'll take her home with me."

"Come, Natasha, you'll wait for them there. We'll watch from the window."

Nettie turned. It was Josie's mother. "I can't," she said. "I've got to find Cassie." She broke away, the coat falling from her shoulders.

Nettie hid from Josie's mother, whose voice, rising above all the others, called out to her. Nettie thought only of finding Cassie. And when the fire was finally under control, and the last of the hoses had been dragged out, she found her.

"Sorry, young lady," a voice said, placing a limp, wet

Cassie into her arms. He shook his head. "She must have gotten stuck trying to get out the window."

Nettie held Cassie close. She had to do something. Cassie needed to be rubbed down. She needed to drink some warm milk. Needed to have her fur brushed.

Nettie dashed toward the door, but hands grasped her shoulders. Stopped her. "Nobody's going in there till the captain has cleared the area.

"But I've got to dry Cassie. Get her warm."

"Little lady, that cat's lived all of its nine lives." The fireman took his hat off and rubbed his forehead, put his hat back on and held out his arms. "Let me have her," he said, his voice soft and kind. "I'll take care of things."

Nettie pulled Cassie closer.

"Don't be scared. I'm just trying to help. When my little guy's dog died —"

"Don't say that. Don't. Pa says cats are surefooted —"

The screech of tires, a loud thump, wheels hitting the curb, and then Pa's voice. "God Almighty —

"Take your hands off me." His cries echoed the sound of the tires. "Let me go —"

He pushed one fireman and then another until he freed himself, cleared a path, and ran inside, the firemen behind him. Nettie heard his cries, seeping from every window, breaking through every wall. "God help me. Help me. Do not do this. God damn it, take me. Take me now —"

And then as though Nettie was watching a horror movie, she saw Pa being carried out. One fireman at his head, one at his feet. They laid him down gently. Rubbed his hands. Slapped his face.

Nettie wanted to squeeze her eyes shut the way she did in the movies, or hide under a seat until the scary part passed. She tried to call out to Pa but nothing came from her lips.

"Clear the area. Give this man some air."

"Natasha. Please. You must come." Again Josie's mother wrapped her coat around Nettie. "Your grandfather —"

"Stop," Nettie shouted, tossing the coat from her shoulders. "Let me go —" She clutched Cassie to her and ran past Josie's mother, past the firemen, past the fire trucks, running down one street and then another.

The sun disappeared and a light rain began to fall. The wind from the harbor blew in. The rain came down harder. Nettie tucked Cassie under her blouse, kept her close to her chest, tried to keep her warm, murmured over and over, "You'll be all right. Pa, too. He'll be fine. Yes, he will."

But Cassie was cold and still; Nettie, wet, tired, afraid. She turned, thinking she heard a voice. Maybe John Peter's. But he wasn't there. Nobody was. And yet, she heard something. Someone. But she was alone on the wet, empty sidewalk, only the sound of cars humming along the street, splashing bits of rain on her legs and feet. Cassie's paw fell from under her blouse.

Icy shivers ran through Nettie and then a strange thing happened. The rain stopped and the sky brightened. And again, she thought she heard someone. "Who is it?" Nettie whispered. "Where are you?" She walked through a gate and into a garden, and beyond the garden she saw a church. St. Leonard's.

Nettie had been to St. Leonard's just once, but she didn't go inside. John Peter had gone in with the grandfather, but she wouldn't. Couldn't. But now she walked slowly up the path leading to the entrance. She climbed the stairs, opened the heavy oak door, and went inside. All along the walls, candles flickered in small vases. Great golden pillars lined the aisles. Nettie made her way down the center aisle and sat in a side pew. Gently, oh so gently, she took Cassie from under her blouse and laid her across her lap.

She rubbed Cassie's belly lightly, slowly. Then harder and faster. Over Cassie's back. Harder and harder. Faster and faster. She wrapped her fingers around Cassie's tail, that soft, silky tail now stiff in her hand. The iciest shiver shot through Nettie. "I'm sorry," she whispered. "So sorry, Pa."

An eerie hum came from deep inside Nettie's throat, then a cry, then sobs that racked her body. Echoing around the church, echoing until the sobs became a wail. Then silence.

She sat for a long time, Cassie across her lap. Hot tears filled her eyes, slid down her cheeks, making everything shimmer and glisten so that the figures in one of the stained glass windows seemed to move. Nettie rubbed her eyes, blinked, looked at other windows. But their figures were still.

Cupping her blouse, she made a sling for Cassie and walked slowly across the aisle and stood beneath the window. The late afternoon sun coming through the window made a rainbow of color. Pale yellows and pinks. Blues and greens. It lit up the figures, especially their faces. Below, in bold letters, Nettie finally saw what she had refused to see with Pa and John Peter.

In Memory of

ELIZABETH WHITEHALL DE ANGELUS

JOHN PETER DE ANGELUS

ANNA BIANCA DE ANGELUS

Nettie reached up and ran her hands over the figures. Finally letting go of Grandma Bessie's warning that only crazy people talk to the dead, she spoke to them.

"Momma? Poppa? It's Nettie. Can you hear me? Cassie is dead. Pa's hurt. And it's my fault. He told me not to light the stove. I always lit the stove. I did. I even made the fire at Grandma Bessie's. I did everything I was supposed to do. I took care of John Peter. I just wanted to help. Momma. Poppa."

From a distance, Nettie heard something. Voices? Yes. Not like she heard Pa and John Peter. And not words she could hear with her ears. But she knew they were there. The cold shivers that shot through her left, leaving a warm glow that surrounded her like a circle of light. "Momma," she whispered. "Momma —"

Hands enveloped Nettie's shoulders. Pa's hands. She

knew that before she lifted her head and looked at him. His face was sooty and two tear tracks lined his cheeks. "They heard me," she whispered.

He nodded. His hands dug deep into her shoulders. "I thought I lost you. I thought I lost John —"

"Cassie is . . . dead. It's my fault."

He shook his head. "She was old. Weary. And perhaps she got tired of waiting for Anna to pass by."

He looked up at the window. "Do you remember when you first came and I talked to Anna all the time?"

Nettie stroked Cassie's back; tears started again.

"But now I talk to her less, because I have you and John." He smiled a slow, sweet smile, reached up, and touched Anna's name. "But even now, in the night before I sleep, I speak to her."

They stood, their breath the only sound, Nettie's eyes fixed on the window until the last bit of sun that rested on her mother's name disappeared.

"Now come." the grandfather placed his coat on Nettie's shoulders. "It is time to get you into warm clothes." He gently pulled Cassie's ear, rubbed his finger under her chin, and tucked a coat sleeve around her. "Tomorrow, old friend, we will take care of you."

⊰ Chapter Twenty-four ⊱

The fire wasn't as bad as it looked the day it happened. Most of the damage was from smoke, except the kitchen. Everything was destroyed there. The sitting room, too. And even though the bedrooms were just filled with soot, it was not possible to stay.

But things worked out. With borrowed beds and linens, and Josie's parents' basement apartment, they set up a temporary home. It was tiny and cramped, but nobody seemed to mind, least of all Nettie. They were together.

Nettie told the grandfather she would get a job after school and during the summer to pay for all that had been lost. But the grandfather said it wouldn't be necessary. That Josie's uncle had asked him to help him with his business. "When he has too many funerals to handle, I will take over."

At first Nettie hated the thought of it. Coming to terms with her parents' death was one thing; having bodies downstairs was another. But the grandfather would hear none of her ideas on what other business he could get into, reminding her once again that she was the child, he the one in charge: "The funeral business is what I know and that is what I will do."

The night after the fire, they buried Cassie. The grandfather wrapped her in one of Anna's lace pillowcases and placed her in one of her hatboxes. John Peter offered his cigar box. The grandfather thanked him, told him he knew how much the box meant to him, but said he thought Cassie might want to be in something belonging to Anna. "She was Anna's cat from the day she came to our door."

Even though it was an unwritten rule that pets were not to be buried in a people cemetery, they did just that. Josie's uncle drove them in one of the limousines and waited at the gate. John Peter and Nettie worked quickly by the light of Pa's flashlight and when they finished digging, they placed Cassie gently in the ground and said good-bye. Then Nettie took John Peter's hand, whispered that Pa should be alone, and led him back to where Josie's uncle waited.

They moved back home when things were ready. Pa got busy with his business, Nettie with school and rehearsals, John Peter practicing his lines. He'd been chosen to announce the concert. He didn't stutter anymore. Not with anybody. Nettie didn't miss the poking and whispering; she was happy for him.

The night of the concert, Nettie was so nervous she could barely button the back of her dress. Her dress. It

150

was beautiful. Pa had taken her shopping, letting her pick out any dress she wanted. "Up to twenty-five dollars," he'd said.

She tried to tame the curls that refused to be tamed, took the lipstick Josie borrowed from her mother, and put just enough on, the way she remembered her mother doing.

"You are beautiful, Natasha," the grandfather said when she came into the kitchen. As always, the radio was on and music filled the apartment. He held out his arms. "May I have this dance?"

Nettie could feel her cheeks redden. She shook her head.

"No?" He walked toward her. "I say yes." He took her hand in his. "I promise I will not step on your feet."

Nettie reached up and put her hand on his shoulder. And they danced. Around the kitchen table. Down the narrow hall past pictures of people long gone. Past John Peter's room, John Peter so deep into rehearsing his lines, he didn't see them go by. Into the parlor.

The sweetest feeling washed over Nettie. One she remembered feeling many times at Morgan Creek. She closed her eyes and saw her mother and father in the distance, the early evening sky a rainbow of color. Baby John Peter high up on her father's shoulders. A small Nettie trailing along behind them.

When she opened her eyes, they were gone, but the warm, safe feeling wasn't. She thought of all the years she wouldn't accept their death, thinking if she did, they really would be gone from her forever. But now, she knew they would be with her always.

Like Pa. Not sitting in the window, waiting. But there. She looked up at him. He looked serious and sad, even though there was a tiny smile on his face.

"What are you thinking about?"

He sighed a very long sigh, longer than Nettie had ever sighed. "How lucky I am." He looked up. "I am, Anna. I am."

John Peter burst into the room. "Who's going to go over this with me —" And then, the biggest smile Nettie had ever seen him smile lit up John Peter's face. "I didn't know you could dance, Pa."

"And why not? Am I not Natasha Allegra of the angels' grandpère?"

John Peter had told. In the beginning she would have killed him. Knocked him to the ground. But today, as she twirled under Pa's outstretched arm one final time, Nettie laughed.

Mrs. Gardner's museum was all Nettie knew it would be, and the concert was all she hoped it would be. She sang without hitting one wrong note, her voice pure and sweet. She kept her eyes on Pa the way he told her to do. "Sing to one person. Forget the others. You will be fine."

John Peter had done fine, too. Nettie listened as he introduced each soloist, and when it came to her turn, her stomach threw itself into a knot. She stood in the wings, Josie beside her, wishing the night was over. "Come on," Josie said, "you're on." She smoothed the back of Nettie's dress, gave her a gentle push toward the stage, and said, "You can do it. You can do anything. You're the miracle worker." She pointed to her mother sitting in the audience. "You got Mama out of the window."

When the applause stopped and the lights came up, and people left the hall, Nettie stood for a few moments, hoping to commit to memory every single minute of this night — every detail of the hall, the stage, the music — the way she'd always done, as though good things might not happen again. But now she knew better. She'd be back.

"Come on, Nettie," John Peter called. "Pa says we're going for gelati at Umberto's. Josie and everybody are going to meet us there."

Nettie slipped her hand into the grandfather's; John Peter took the other. They walked around the parapet, the court and gardens below them, down the stone staircase, through the cloisters and out into the mild spring night.

They decided to walk the long way to the subway that would take them home. Work up an appetite for Umberto's gelati, the grandfather said. The streetlights glowed, cars tooted their horns all along the avenue. Nettie remembered the first night they'd come. The loneliness. The fear of not being wanted, of being sent back to Grandma Bessie's. And now, tonight, Josie waiting for her at Umberto's with her mother and father. Donnie, too.

Pa, here with her, walking down the avenue. All of them wanting her and John Peter. Pa needing them. Loving them. They *were* a family. Not the big, happy family Aleta said they were. But a family.

Stuffed with gelati and cappuccino and cookies, they made their way home, and when they got there, Nettie asked if they could go up to the roof. She and Josie sometimes did their homework up there, but Nettie had never been on the roof at night.

Nettie talked on about the concert. How beautiful the museum was. How good the gelati were.

"And what about Donnie's mother," John Peter said. "She came."

The grandfather spoke of their grandmother. Of Cassie. Of their father. What a good boy he'd been. How gentle he was with everyone. How he could still see him up on the roof, caring for the neighbor's pigeons.

The moon was full and the sky was dotted with stars. Nettie remembered how when she first came, she thought she would never see the moon and the stars again. And now, here on the roof, on Salem Street, the light of the moon lit up the tiny silvery particles on the roof's shingles, so there were stars at her feet, too.

After a while, Pa said it was time they got to bed. John Peter fussed a bit but started down the narrow, winding stairs leading to the hall below. Nettie followed, the grandfather behind her.

"John Peter," Nettie said, "you were right about Grandma Bessie."

154

"What do you mean?"

"Remember when you said she must have loved us a little?"

He turned and looked up at her. "Because she sent us the cookies?"

"I brought the cookies. But she did love us and I'll bet it was more than a little?"

"Why do you say that?"

"Because she sent us home." Nettie reached back and took the grandfather's hand. "She sent us to Pa."